Jen McLaughlin

Manufactured in the United States of America

ISBN: 978-0-9896684-1-5

The author acknowledges the copyrighted or trademarked status and trademark owners of the following wordmarks mentioned in this work of fiction: Saran Wrap, Rolex, G-Shock, McDonald's, Islands, Marines, Men in Black, LAX, iPhone, Starbucks, Ferrari, Harley Davidson, National Lampoon's Christmas Vacation, Glock, Skype, Monopoly, Gmail, Ritz, Town Car, Perry Como, Google, Channing Tatum, Kim Kardashian, Candy Crush, and Downton Abbey.

Edited by: Coat of Polish Edits

Copy edited by: Hollie Westring at hollietheeditor.com

Cover Designed by: Sarah Hansen at © OkayCreations.net

Interior Design and Formatting by: E.M. Tippetts Book Designs

OUT OF TIME

This one is for Tessa, Jill, and Trent. You guys kept me sane during my writing spree, and you're the best friends a girl could ask for.

Desperate to keep him...

I've finally gotten everything I ever wanted: love, freedom, happiness, and, most importantly, Finn. Our love is everything I expected it to be and more. We've finally found each other, but the world seems determined to tear us apart. We thought my father was the only obstacle between us, but now it's the military. With Finn's departure looming, we're squeezing in every moment together before we run out of time.

Trying to make every moment count...

Being Carrie's bodyguard was one thing. Being her boyfriend is another. Every day she's mine is a day the sun shines in my life. Yet our time together is running out. Her father will never think a tattooed Marine will be good enough, so I'll do whatever it takes to be worthy of her love. But the road will take me away from the girl who makes me feel alive—the girl I can't live without.

Time only gets us so far...

Never letting go…

He closed his arms around me and carried me to his bed. He was so hard and solid and it drove me insane every time he moved his tongue over mine like that. His teeth scraped my lower lip, and I whimpered into his mouth. His fingers moved over my butt, slipping between my legs and rubbing against the spot where I needed him most.

As he lowered me to the mattress, he started to climb on top of me, but I broke the kiss and shoved at his shoulders. "No," I said, locking gazes with him. "It's my turn. Just stand there."

He stilled, instantly giving me what I wanted. "Your turn for what?"

"Control," I said, my cheeks heating. "I want to undress you."

He fisted his hands at his hips, watching me from beneath his lowered lids. When he looked at me like that—like I was his dessert or something—it made everything inside of me quiver and beg for his touch so much it hurt. I licked my lips and crawled to the edge of the bed on all fours. He twitched and took a step toward me; as if he couldn't hold himself back anymore, but then he stopped.

He stood there because I'd asked him to.

I ran my hands over his chest, then up over his shoulders. Just touching him made me feel like the luckiest girl in the world, and I wanted to do everything to him. Everything in the romance books I read at night, and then *more*. Even though my mother had never figured it out, I used to sneak them out of her library after she was finished with them. I'd started it in sixth grade. Now I bought them with my own money.

And I had a lot of ideas stored away in my mind that I wanted to try out on Finn.

CHAPTER ONE

Finn

I pulled Carrie tighter to my chest, closing my eyes, even though I was fully awake and alert. I just needed a second to hold her. To breathe her in. I wanted to ignore life for a second longer, because today was the day I had to tell Carrie I have bad news, and I was not looking forward to it. But hell, I didn't even necessarily know what the message was about yet. Maybe I was jumping to conclusions.

Maybe I was full of shit. Or…maybe it was bad news.

The sun came through the curtains, and I opened my eyes again, sighing. When I had woken up earlier, my first conscious thought had been: *Please don't let this all be a dream again. Please don't make me wake up alone.*

But then I'd breathed in her familiar scent that instantly calmed my racing heart, and I had relaxed again. It hadn't been a dream. Thank fucking God. The real world was just as happy as my dreams—which made sense since she starred in both anyway. The woman I loved had forgiven me for secretly working for her father and all was right in the world. Her bright blue eyes were shut tight, her long red hair lay splayed all across her white pillow, and her soft lips seemed to be begging to be kissed.

Her ginger eyelashes were swept low, shadowing her pale cheeks. If someone would have told me last week that Carrie would be back in my

1

bed, in my arms, and in love with me, I would have laughed and asked them what the fuck they were smoking.

Yet here she was. *This* was real.

And she was late for class.

"Ginger...?"

I kissed her lips, savoring the unique flavor that was my Carrie. I made sure not to press too close to her, though, and give her the wrong idea. Or maybe it was myself I was trying to remind. But either way, there wasn't any time for a quick morning fuck.

I pulled back, and her lids fluttered open, showing me those baby blues I loved so much. "Hey," she said, her voice soft with sleep.

"It's time to wake up."

She smiled up at me, stretching like a cat. "Why are you all the way over there?"

I trailed my finger down the little strip of skin on her stomach, right above her green panties. Would I ever get sick of seeing little pieces of her skin bared for me and only me? "Because you're—"

Without warning, she snaked her arms around my neck, hauling me closer until I lay on top of her. So much for keeping my distance. Her hands played with the back of my hair. I loved it when she did that, and I had a feeling she knew it. She could ask me to walk along hot coals for her, and as long as she was playing with my hair like that, I'd do it happily.

Without hesitation, she kissed me, her tongue slipping inside my mouth and entwining with mine. Damn it, I loved it when she took the initiative, but I had to stop this before it went too far. I pulled back and unwound her arms from my neck. Then I scooted out of her reach. "You're late for class."

She sat upright, blinking rapidly. "I am?"

"Yep." I rolled out of bed, and away from the woman who held my heart in her hands. "You get in the shower, and I'll make you breakfast to go."

"Thank you," she called over her shoulder, bolting toward the bathroom in her tank top and satin underwear. I had to pause to appreciate the back view, but then I hightailed it into the kitchen to make her an egg sandwich.

I passed my phone as I went, snatching it up, and quickly called her a cab before setting it down on the counter. As I made her breakfast, I eyed the fucking thing as if it was going to jump up and bite me in the ass. Sometimes, I felt like it could. It had been the root of all bad things that happened to me lately.

First it had shown Carrie I was a liar. Then the call last night…

Nothing was definite yet. Nothing at all. But when you got a mysterious phone call from your commanding officer on a Sunday night…well, you could put two and two together pretty easily. In this fucked-up world, someone was always a finger push away from starting a war with *someone*. And who were the first ones sent in?

Marines. Always the Marines.

But some small, stupid part of me couldn't help but hope the call was nothing more than a red herring. God had a twisted sense of humor like that, didn't He? It seemed like something He would do. Give me the sun and the moon, and then pretend like he was going to snatch away the sun. Then, at the last second, he'd laugh and be all, *"Ha! I got you, didn't I?"*

I shook my head at myself. Was I seriously having a fake fucking conversation with God in my head? I was losing it. Losing my mind. I needed to look at this rationally.

Maybe the military thought there would be another attack in Egypt or something and were readying troops just in case. There were a hell of a lot of *just in case* situations in the military. It didn't have to *mean* something.

The possible threat could fail to come to fruition. Then I'd get to stay with Carrie.

It's not that I was scared to go fight for my country. I wasn't. But I *was* scared of how Carrie would handle the news of me going. That's not to say I didn't think she was strong enough to handle it, because she was. She just worried about me.

I flipped the egg and popped some bread into the toaster. As I waited, I eyed my phone and replayed the message in my head. Screw this. I needed to hear it again. I picked it up and hit *play*.

"Sergeant Coram, this is C.O. Gunnerson. Report for duty at Pendleton Saturday morning at oh-eight-hundred, and be advised there will be news regarding a possible deployment for you in the near future."

The commanding officer's gravelly voice rang in my head, making me want to throw the phone across the room. But, instead, I slammed it down on the countertop, my heart thumping loudly. Yeah. That didn't sound good at all.

I shouldn't be surprised. This was a pattern in my life. The second things started to look up for me, shit always blew up in my face. Like the time I'd gotten the job of my dreams, only to learn it would require me to travel out of the country for ten months of the year. Or the time I'd gotten my Harley, and then an asshole in a pickup truck smashed it into pieces.

This certainly wasn't the first time I'd gone through this type of thing, and it wouldn't be the last.

The toast popped and I set it down on the Saran Wrap. After putting the rest of her sandwich together, I poured her a to-go mug of coffee and waited at the door. She came charging out of the bathroom with jeans and my t-shirt on; her hair in a sloppy ponytail. Hot damn, I didn't want to let her walk out the door.

But I knew I had to.

She grabbed her bag, slung it over her shoulder, and came my way. "You giving me a ride?"

I raised a brow. "Can you eat and drink coffee on a bike?"

"No."

"Then no." I kissed her quickly, not wanting to hold her up even more, and handed her the coffee. Her fingers brushed against mine, and I wanted to capture them and hold them close to my chest. Right above my heart. "I called you a cab, and it's out there waiting for you."

She grinned at me, her warm eyes shining up at me. "Thanks, love."

"*Love?*" I scratched my head. "That's new."

She shrugged and took the sandwich from me. "I'm trying it on for size. You have so many nicknames for me, it's only fair I think of one for you."

"Hm." I patted her on the ass, the universal signal to get going. "Well, *Ginger*, I'll pick you up after class. Five, right?"

"Yes." Her cheeks flushed, and her gaze dipped to my mouth. "I have to study afterward with a friend, so make it six?"

"Which friend?"

"A new one you don't know." She kissed me. "A girl. She's majoring in biology, too, with the end goal of occupational therapy. Just like me."

"Ah. I suppose I'll share then." I slapped her ass gently. "Off you go."

Her eyes darkened. "Do I *have* to go?"

"You know you do. If your grades fail, then I do, too."

She huffed. "I *had* to go and fall for the guy whose job it is to make sure I don't fail, didn't I?"

"Don't look so sad. If you hurry up and get to class—*and* behave yourself all day—maybe I'll help you study again."

She perked up at that. "Deal."

I pulled her in for one last kiss. "I love you, Ginger."

"I love you, too."

I watched her climb down the stairs and make her way toward the yellow taxi. She took a sip of her coffee and slid into the cab, her eyes on me as she pulled away. Once she was out of sight, I sighed and went back inside. As I made myself a sandwich and brewed another cup of coffee, I picked up my phone and unlocked it.

Two texts already.

Ever since I got sent here to guard her—babysit her, more like—I'd been on a daily text routine with her fucking father. He was like a needy teenager in some ways. If I didn't immediately text him first thing in the morning, I got at least three texts before I could finish my coffee. The funny thing was she didn't even need watching.

Well, maybe she did a little bit.

Only because she'd gone and fallen in love with me, despite my initial lies about my real identity and the fact I was her father's lackey sent to spy on her. But no one was going to take her from me—not even her dad. I needed her too badly.

She reported to class on time.

Barely thirty seconds passed before the phone buzzed again. *Good. Check on her after and make sure you actually text me back.*

I snorted. *Will do, sir.*

After I sent the text, I spun the phone in my hand, debating my next move. Maybe I should call Dad and see what he thought was up. He'd been in the military long enough to get how things ran. I could practically hear his voice now. He'd say something along the lines of, "*Griffin, you know what this is as well as I do. You're going to war, son.*"

Maybe I would check in with one of my squad members. See if they knew something I didn't. After flipping my egg in the nick of time, I dialed my buddy Hernandez.

"Hello?" Hernandez said, his voice rough.

"Hey. It's Coram."

Hernandez set something down. Maybe his coffee mug? "What's up, man?"

"Did you get a call last night?"

"From who?"

I leaned against the counter. "Our C.O.?"

"Um, no." Hernandez cleared his throat. "Should I have? What's going on?"

"Shit, I don't know. I thought…" I rubbed my forehead, but it did nothing to take away the ache between my eyes. "Fuck me."

"No thanks," Hernandez said. "You're not my type."

I snorted. "The hell I'm not."

"Yeah…no. I prefer blondes. But why would he call you and not me?"

I shook my head. "I got a call from him that I have to show up this weekend. But if I'm the only one, what the fuck does that mean?"

"I don't know." I heard a door shut. "I hung out with Smith last night, and he didn't mention it either. So I don't know, man."

So two people hadn't gotten the call, but I had? What the fuck did that mean? It didn't make any sense. "All right. Thanks, man."

"Do you think they—?" A muffled knock sounded through the phone. "Shit. I gotta go, Coram. I'll call you later."

"Yeah. Sure."

I hung up the phone and set it down, my head hurting even more now. So I wasn't being deployed with my unit, but I might be deploying soon?

None of this made any sense, damn it.

CHAPTER TWO

Later that day, I shoved all my school crap into my brown messenger bag. I'd just finished my study session with my partner from chemistry, and still had a crapload of homework to do, but that was hardly a surprise. Going to school to become an occupational therapist was not an easy thing.

With it came tons of homework and labs and studying. I'd known it was what I wanted to do since I'd entered high school, and I hadn't wavered from it at all. I loved helping people, so it seemed like a good fit for me to pick a career where I was, well, helping people. Hands down.

But now I was finding that juggling a love life and school and lying to Dad about it was a *bit* hard to keep up with. Not that I was complaining or anything. It was a lot to handle sometimes. Tonight before I left, I needed to drop off a few articles of clothing in the main room so people could take what they wanted, then I also had to grab a change of clothes for me.

I had a feeling I would be spending the night at Finn's house again, and that was A-okay with me, thank you very much. Heck, if I had it my way, I'd never leave his side again except for school. Even that was a challenge, to be honest.

I knew I had to focus on studies, and so I did. There wasn't a question of me slacking in that area. I had goals and dreams, and they didn't include flunking out of college. But it was better when Finn was with me. I even slept better with him beside me. I *needed* him there, being all hot, smart-assy, annoying, and irresistible all at once.

You know. Being Finn.

When I'd found out he was my father's spy *after* falling in love with him, I never would've thought we could move on from that. Never thought *I* could move on from that. But when it came to a life without Finn, well, I didn't want to live that life.

I'd tried it. It sucked. I wasn't going back.

I heard someone come up behind me in the library and I gazed over my shoulder. One of the last people I wanted to talk to right now stood there, looking ashamed of himself.

Good. He should be.

"Hey, Carrie."

He scratched his head, barely managing to muss up his blond hair, and gave me a sheepish smile. His gold Rolex—which almost made me laugh, since Finn called him Golden Boy—glinted in the light, so at contrast with Finn's G-Shock watch he sometimes wore that it made me wonder what the hell I'd ever thought Cory could give me out of life. He was my politician father about thirty years ago.

I had no idea why there'd even been a hint of interest in my mind for this man when Finn was within a five hundred-mile radius of me. Cory was everything my father would want for me, and everything I did *not*.

I tensed. "Hi."

"Uh…" Cory cleared his throat. "Can we talk about the other night? I saw you over here studying earlier, but didn't want to interrupt."

I was trying to forget all about that ugly scene outside of the frat party where he said those awful things to Finn about him being nothing more than trailer park trash. *Really* freaking hard. It was kind of difficult to be the bigger person when I wanted to punch him for being so darn condescending to the man I loved.

No one insulted Finn and got away with it. Call me overprotective, and maybe I was more like Dad than I cared to admit, but I wanted to claw out Cory's eyes.

I blew my hair out of my face and shoved my last book into my bag. It barely fit. "I don't really think there's anything to say."

"Look," Cory said quietly, his eyes lowered, "I'm sorry that I—"

"How's your stomach, by the way?"

Cory flushed and shifted on his feet. "It's fine. I don't even really remember what happened that night. I was pretty drunk."

"Yeah, I kind of noticed." I headed down the stairs to the classroom's exit, and he walked with me. "You said some pretty nasty things, you know."

He stopped walking. "To you?"

"To Finn." I looked at him out of the corner of my eye.

He totally relaxed when I told him it wasn't me he hurt. The jerk.

Cory rubbed the back of his neck. For his part, he did at least look slightly ashamed of what he'd done. "I really don't recall. I just remember waking up with a sore stomach and a copy of the police report I apparently filed. I feel horrible about the whole thing. You have to believe me."

"I'm sure you do," I said, gripping the shoulder strap of my bag even tighter. My anger faded away a little bit, but not all the way. "He'll be outside waiting for me, so you can apologize to him if you want."

He flushed and stumbled on a step. "Are you two…you know, back together?"

"Yeah, we are." I pressed my lips together, feeling as if I needed to explain myself or something. "I know you thought we were—"

He laughed uneasily, but his red cheeks gave away his discomfiture on the topic. "I didn't think anything. Really. It's fine. I hope you're happy with him. That's all that matters."

"No speeches about how it'll fail this time?"

He lifted a shoulder and averted his eyes. "I think I said enough on this topic already, don't you?"

"I guess you did, yeah."

He opened the door for me and motioned me through. Today he seemed different. I lifted my head, squinting through the bright sun for any signs of Finn. And then I saw him.

He leaned against a huge palm tree, his bike parked behind him. He wore a pair of ripped blue jeans and a green T-shirt with a stick figure missing his back on the front. The other figure held it in his hand and smiled. It was funny and stupid and so *Finn*.

His tattoos flexed on his muscular arms, making me want to trace each one with my tongue, and I took a big step toward him.

Would that urge, that *need* for him, ever go away?

God, I hoped not.

I knew the exact moment he noticed me. His eyes warmed, and he ran his left hand over his short brown curls. His mouth tipped into a bright smile…that is, until his gaze skidded to the side and he noticed who was with me.

Then he looked less sunny and more dangerous. Go figure.

He tugged on his curls and he pushed off the tree, stalking toward me. As he crossed the grass, Cory stiffened beside me. "Is he going to hit me again?" he whispered.

"No, he wouldn't do that." I hesitated, watching the storm gather in Finn's blue eyes, making them look almost gray. "I wouldn't say anything cocky, though, if I were you."

"God, no," Cory said, straightening to his full height. "I'm not an idiot."

That might be debatable, but I kept my mouth shut. He'd said he was sorry.

Finn reached us in record time, and he held his hand out for my bag. I gave it to him without a fight. As he slipped it over his own shoulder, he shot Cory a foul look.

"What the hell is Cody doing here?" Finn snapped, his entire body throwing off anger in heat waves.

I didn't bother to correct him about Cory's name. He knew darn well he'd said it wrong. I walked over to his side and rested a hand on his chest. "Finn, let him talk."

"Why should I?" His heart thumped erratically beneath my hand, and he looked down at me, the anger softening slightly. "I've got nothing to say to him."

"Because he has something to say to you." I moved to Finn's side, entwining his fingers with mine. Finn held on, his grip firm. "Cory, go ahead."

"I'm…" Cory looked at me, pale. I nodded, giving him the encouragement he seemed to need. "I'm s-sorry I was a jerk the other night. Whatever I said…I didn't mean it."

"Oh, but I think you did." Finn snorted. "Maybe, for the first time in your entire life, you were completely honest with me."

Cory flushed. "Seeing as how I don't even remember what I said, I can't agree or disagree."

"Let me enlighten you. You said that—"

I nudged Finn with my elbow a little harder than necessary. I could tell he was itching for a fight and would gladly give it to Cory if given the slightest provocation. "*Finn.*"

"Fine." He sighed and smiled at Cory, but it came across as more predatory than friendly. "You're forgiven. I won't punch you, and you can go back to silently hating me and waiting for Carrie and me to fall apart. Deal?"

Cory choked on a laugh and took a step back from us. "Uh, yeah. Sure. Whatever you say, man."

Finn narrowed his eyes at Cory. I tugged on his hand, trying to distract him, and started talking way too fast. "Well, now that that's over and everyone is friends again…" Finn still didn't look away from Cory, and Cory was growing paler by the second. I tugged harder. "Hello? Earth to Finn."

Finn finally looked down at me, his hot eyes searing into mine. He seemed to shake off whatever he'd been thinking. "Yeah. I'm here."

"Good." I smiled at him, my heart skipping a beat when he placed his hand on the small of my back. His hard chest pressed against mine, making me want to press closer and rub up against him like a stripper doing a lap dance. "You ready?"

"Hell yeah," Finn said, leading me toward his bike. He glanced over his shoulder, his brow furrowed, and his eyes on where Cory probably still stood. "That took a lot more self-control than I thought I had, I'll have you know."

"Why?"

"I don't like him."

"I know, but he's harmless enough."

"Yeah." Finn snorted. "As harmless as a sniper."

I looked back at Cory. He wore a lavender shirt, was going to school to become a doctor, and had manicured nails. He turned and walked away, his stride slow and laid-back, just like he was. Call me crazy, but that didn't exactly scream *dangerous thug* to me. "I just don't see what you see."

"It's simple, really. He likes you. I don't like him," Finn said, grabbing my helmet off the bike. "Need I say more?"

He stuck my helmet under the crook of his elbow and smoothed my hair from my face. With his hands on either side of my head, he leaned down and pressed his mouth to mine, stealing my breath away with a simple kiss. My stomach twisted in knots, and my heart thudded in my ears.

When he pulled back, he ran his thumb over my lower lip and gave me a small smile. The way my body reacted to the simple touch, he might as well have stripped naked in the street. His blue eyes skimmed over my body, making me tense with anticipation. "Were you a good girl today?"

"Of course I was," I answered instantly. "When am I *not*?"

"If you got down on your knees with my cock in your mouth," he said, his gaze fastened on my mouth. "You'd be pretty damned bad then."

"*Finn.*"

My cheeks heated and so did other parts of my body. Namely, in between my legs. I'd be lucky if I made it home before jumping his bones. And man, I wanted to do what he described now that he'd put the image in my head.

I wanted to kneel at his feet and taste him with my tongue, sucking him in deeper and deeper until he came in my—

"Hello?" He waved his hand in front of my face, his lips curved into a smile. "Did I break you?"

I licked my lips and he watched me hungrily, his gaze flashing as he read my expression. "Nope, not broken. I want to go home and do exactly what you just said, so hurry the heck up, will you?"

His eyes widened. "Fuck yeah." He slid the helmet over my head, slammed his own on, and climbed onto the bike. "Climb on."

Oh, I wanted to. And I would…as soon as I got rid of some clothes. It was the perfect time to do it, because most of my dorm mates were at dinner. "Hold on. I need two minutes."

I grabbed the bundle of shirts I was donating, ran inside my building, and threw the clothes in the normal spot. Mom sent me way too many clothes, so I shared. No biggie. I darted back outside without being seen.

As I got on the bike behind him, I let my hands dip lower to his erection. Man, he was hard and ready and *mine*. He revved the bike and hissed when I closed my hand over him through his jeans. "Fuck, Ginger, keep that up and we won't even make it home."

"Then drive fast," I said, resting my head on his shoulder. "Now."

The tires squealed as we pulled away from the curb, and I laughed.

When we got home, I planned on doing all the things I'd been dying to do since this morning. If I had it my way, we wouldn't even say a freaking word once we cleared his door.

I needed him too badly.

I closed my eyes, enjoying the air whipping around us as he buzzed through the crowded streets, darting in between stopped cars as if we were invincible. And lately I'd been feeling pretty darn invincible. I felt like I could handle anything life threw at me from now on.

I had a freedom I'd never had before. My lifelong goals were all laid out and in motion, including acing classes and having a great GPA. I was making more and more friends every day. And to top it off, I had a hot, surfing, tattooed, bike-riding Marine for a boyfriend.

Even better? He loved me as much as I loved him.

We *were* invincible.

As long as we had each other.

CHAPTER THREE

Finn

As soon as I turned off the bike, she was standing and removing her helmet. After I took it from her, she held her hand out to me. The image of her there, the sun setting behind her and silhouetting her perfectness, was so fucking beautiful that I wanted to take a picture of it and carry it with me wherever I went.

I was never one for taking pictures, but she had changed a lot of things about me. Now I *talked* and *forgave* instead of kicking ass and asking questions later. Now I was a fucking softie, and I didn't even mind.

If I had a camera in my pocket, I'd have snapped it right then and there. But no one carried around cameras anymore. Not with cell phones.

No shit, Sherlock. Use the fucking phone.

"Don't move a muscle. Don't even twitch a finger." I hung the helmets on my bike and took out my phone, grinning at her. "Hey. I saw you blink."

She shifted on her feet. "Blinking is kind of essential. Are you taking a picture of me?"

"Yep." I grinned. "Isn't that what boyfriends do?" I opened the camera app. "Take pictures and set it as their backgrounds or some shit like that?"

She laughed and I snapped the picture. She still was silhouetted perfectly, but she was smiling. Fucking perfect. Her hand dropped. "Let me see it."

"Nope. It's all mine." I shoved the phone into my pocket and grabbed her hand, hauling her up against me. She rested her palm over my heart and I smiled down at her, so fucking happy it hurt. "Just like you are."

She opened her mouth to talk, but I didn't let her. Instead, I trapped her mouth under mine, swallowing the words. My mind returned to the odd phone call I'd gotten earlier. I'd called three more members of my unit, and none of them had gotten a call. Just me. I didn't know what to expect or what it meant, but I needed to tell her about it.

Where were they sending me? And why? How long would I be gone? I had all these unanswered questions in my head, and it was driving me fucking insane. If they sent me away, I couldn't be Carrie's bodyguard. And if I wasn't *here*, I couldn't be with Carrie.

If I didn't have Carrie to kiss every single morning…then who the hell was I? I wasn't sure I wanted to know, but I had a feeling I was going to find out.

Her arms wrapped around my neck, dragging me closer, and I deepened the kiss before swinging her into my arms. As I walked up the pathway and up the stairs, I refused to break contact. I needed her as desperately as I had before I'd ever had her.

Maybe even more, if that was possible.

I unlocked my door and kicked it open, then shut it with my hip. Even though I wanted to carry her straight to my bed, I didn't. I needed to tell her about the strange call I'd gotten first. No more secrets. No more waiting.

She tried to kiss me again, but I stepped back and unwound her arms from my neck. "Hold on. We need to talk."

"Why?" She bit down on her lower lip. "What's wrong?"

"Nothing too serious." I cupped her cheek, running my thumb across her lower lip. I loved doing that. Loved seeing her smile, and the faint freckles that danced along her cheekbones when she did. Loved seeing her light up when she helped another person. Loved seeing her on a surfboard. Fuck, I loved *her*. "I got a phone call from my commanding officer. I have to report to base this weekend."

She blinked at me. "But it's the wrong weekend, isn't it?"

"It is." I hesitated and tugged on my hair. I'd have to cut it again. "I don't know what he wants with me, but he mentioned a possible deployment."

She lowered her eyes. "You mean war?"

"I'm not sure yet." I cleared my throat and met her eyes. "The thing is, I called a bunch of guys from my unit, and none of them have to go in. It's just me."

She shook her head. "But what does that mean?"

"I have no fucking clue," I said, reaching up and playing with her hair. I loved the way it felt against my fingers. "It could mean ten million things. I really have no way of knowing until I go and hear the news. But there's definitely *something* going on."

She nodded, her eyes never leaving mine. "Is this a bad thing or a good thing?"

"I really can't say," I said, shrugging. "I can speculate and freak you out with all the what ifs, but until I go and hear the news? It's pointless. I just didn't want to *not* tell you."

"Thank you for being honest right away," she said, after letting out a sigh.

"I won't keep anything from you. Not anymore." I leaned down and kissed her gently, knowing she probably needed a minute to absorb all this. "We're in this together."

She rose up on tiptoe and kissed me, not replying. She curled her hands into my shirt, a desperation in her kiss that hadn't been there before. She was freaking out, and I needed to make it better. I broke off the kiss again, taking a deep breath of air.

"Ginger, it'll be okay."

She nodded, her mouth pressed tight and her eyes narrow. "I know. Just kiss me. I need you to kiss me *now*."

Well, when she put it that way, who was I to say no?

So I kissed her.

Carrie

Okay, I was trying really, really freaking hard not to start panicking.

I mean, he'd said he wasn't going to war, or at least his unit wasn't, so that sounded promising. But still, he'd thrown out the word *deployment*.

I might not know much about the military, but even I knew that meant he'd be leaving me.

And if he was leaving me, I wasn't happy.

When he closed his mouth over mine, I shut off my mind and stopped thinking. He'd already told me all he could tell me about the call, so focusing on it wasn't the healthiest choice. We had to wait until this weekend to hear anything more. Until then we were just sitting ducks.

And if I was going to be forced to wait, then I'd do it my way.

He picked me up and carried me to his bed. He was so hard and solid and it drove me insane every time he moved his tongue over mine like that. His teeth scraped my lower lip, and I whimpered into his mouth. His fingers moved over my butt, slipping between my legs and rubbing against the spot where I needed him most.

As he lowered me to the mattress, he started to climb on top of me, but I broke the kiss and shoved at his shoulders. "No," I said, locking gazes with him. "It's my turn. Just stand there."

He stilled, instantly giving me what I wanted. "Your turn for what?"

"Control," I said, my cheeks heating. "I want to undress you. And then I want to wrap my lips around your...your..."

When I drifted off, uncertain what to call his penis, he chuckled. "Cock. It's a *cock*, Carrie. Say it."

My cheeks heated. I knew what it was called. It just sounded so dirty and wrong. "Around your cock," I said in a rush, my cheeks getting even hotter.

"Okay." He fisted his hands at his hips, watching me from beneath his lowered lids. When he looked at me like that—like I was his dessert or something—it made everything inside me quiver and beg for his touch so much it hurt. I licked my lips and crawled to the edge of the bed on all fours. He twitched and took a step toward me; as if he couldn't hold himself back anymore, but then he stopped.

He stood there because I'd asked him to.

I ran my hands over his chest, then up over his shoulders. Just touching him made me feel like the luckiest girl in the world, and I wanted to do everything to him. Everything in the romance books I read at night, and then *more*. Even though my mother had never figured it out, I used to sneak them out of her library after she was finished with them. I'd started it in sixth grade. Now I bought them with my own money.

And I had a lot of ideas stored away in my mind that I wanted to try out on Finn.

I climbed off the bed and rose on tiptoes, kissing him. His tongue rubbed against mine, making my stomach clench. When I slid my hands down over his pecs and abs and then up under his shirt, he groaned into my mouth. My nails scraped his skin, and I pulled back long enough to pull his shirt over his head.

I stood back and looked at him, his gaze burning into mine as I did so. His dark ink swirled up his arms and over his biceps before it crept over his shoulders and chest. I never got sick of looking at his tattoos. I loved deciphering them and admiring how they intertwined with perfection.

He looked the part of the stereotypical bad boy…when he was anything but.

He was a contradiction at its hottest. I ran my tongue over the black tattoo that swirled over his left pec, grinning when he hissed and gripped my hips. After I nipped at the skin, I pulled back enough to say, "New rule, love. You aren't allowed to wear shirts around me anymore."

"Ever?"

"*Ever.*"

He lifted a shoulder. "It might take some explaining when we go back to D.C., but I bet I can make it work."

"I bet you could, too."

I stepped closer, my leg between his, and tipped my head back to look up at him. His blue eyes shined down at me, and his light brown curls stuck up a bit, probably because I'd run my fingers through them a few times.

His hands still gripped my hips, and they flexed on me. "Ginger…" he said, his tone strained and raspy. The way he sounded, all turned on and needy, washed over me and landed somewhere in my stomach, twisting and turning into a knot. "I'm going to—"

"I know," I said, smiling up at him. "Believe me, I know."

I dropped to my knees and undid the button of his pants. As I unzipped his jeans, he clenched his jaw and closed his eyes, letting me work as slowly as I wanted. It might be torture for him, but I knew he'd let me do whatever the hell I wanted, even if it killed him.

When I pulled down his jeans and let them fall to his feet, he kicked out of them without opening his eyes. Leaning in, I cupped his erection through his boxers, closing my hand around him and squeezing. He hissed and moved his hips back, my hand tight on him. Then he arched into me.

The look of pleasure on his face almost did me in. Touching wasn't enough. He seemed to agree. Reaching down, he yanked off his boxers, and as soon as he was out of my way, I flicked my tongue over the head of his erection.

"Jesus, Carrie." His hands burrowed into my hair and held me in place. "Give me *more*."

I groaned and took him into my mouth, swirling my tongue in circles around him. My God, he felt good there—almost as good as he felt when he was inside me. The skin was so smooth and hard at the same time… and so freaking *intoxicating*. I'd never get enough of him. I took more of him in my mouth, and he looked down at me—his jaw ticking and his body tightly wound.

His blue eyes burned with heated need, and he urged me even closer, his jaw flexing as he arched into my mouth. I closed my eyes and let out a soft moan. The urgent need to be taken by him was growing even stronger. Especially when I tasted the salty tang of something I could only assume was his semen. And I wanted more.

"*Enough*," he said, his voice harsh.

He groaned and lifted me to my feet, crashing his mouth into mine before I could even protest that I hadn't finished. Within seconds, all thoughts of protesting faded away behind the need to be touched. My nails raked over his shoulders, trying to get him even closer to me, and he deepened the kiss until I was flat on my back on the bed. He moved between my thighs, where I needed him so freaking much, and rolled his hips against me.

I might not have control anymore, but I didn't care.

I just needed him.

I wrapped my legs around his waist, but my stupid clothes were in the way. I pulled back and undid my pants, my hands trembling too badly to be fast.

"Hurry up," he growled, ripping them down my legs and tossing them onto the floor. He continued removing my clothing with jerky movements, his hands steady and sure. He stopped when I was in my red bra and lacy red thong. "These can stay."

Without warning, he flipped me onto my stomach and lowered

himself on top of me. It took me a second to adjust to the new position, but then I was ready and willing to move on to the next step. Him—inside of me.

But instead of moving forward to give me what I wanted, he nibbled on my earlobe, biting down just enough to sting. I moaned, the sound escaping from somewhere deep within me. The way he felt, cradling me from behind, drove me insane with want.

"Finn, now." I moved underneath of him restlessly, my whole body humming with desire and electric need. "*Please.*"

He groaned, his hands flexing on my hips, and bit down on my shoulder before licking away the pain. "Fuck, Ginger. I need you so bad."

"Then take me," I breathed, my fingers digging into the mattress and clinging to the comforter. I had a feeling I'd be hanging on for dear life soon. "Right here. Like this."

He moaned. "Not quite yet. You're not ready."

He kissed a path over my shoulder blade, then nibbled on the spot right over my bra clasp. I let out a ragged moan I barely recognized as my own and arched my back. He needed to touch me more. Kiss me more. *Do* more, before I exploded.

He undid my bra and I impatiently threw it to the side, and he cupped my breasts from behind. I cried out when he rolled my nipples in between his fingers, squeezing with the perfect amount of pressure, and my stomach hollowed out.

He rolled his hips against me again, mimicking making love, and I clenched my teeth. He was driving me insane with desire and he wasn't even really *trying*, damn it. I needed…needed…*him*. Now.

He pushed off me and positioned me with my legs spread more widely, but I was still on all fours. I felt extremely exposed in this position, but it was Finn. And with Finn, I could do anything. I studied him from my weird position, watching as desire darkened his gaze. Watched his erection grow even harder and his breathing become even more erratic.

I watched hungrily as he rolled a condom on. He watched me as if I was his reward for good behavior—and I really hoped he never stopped looking at me like that.

He crossed the room, his eyes on my spread thighs. "You might want to hold on tight, Ginger."

I fisted my hands tighter into the comforter when he positioned

21

himself behind me. He slid the small scrap of my lace thong to the side and ran his tongue up my slit. I cried out and dug my knees into the mattress. The shock of pleasure his tongue brought me hit me hard and fast. "Oh my God, Finn."

"You have no idea how fucking beautiful you look right now," he said, his voice so low I barely heard him. I wanted to press my thighs together to ease the empty ache I was feeling without him inside of me, but I couldn't. Not with him in between them. "I bet you want me to taste you again. Don't you?"

"*Yes.*"

He didn't tease me. Didn't waste any time. He flicked his tongue over my clit, then sucked me in between his lips, rolling his tongue perfect circles. When he scraped his teeth against me gently, I cried out and pushed back, demanding more. He gripped my hips with his hands, kneeling behind me and going down on me from behind.

The erotic image this presented made me twitch with pleasure, building higher and higher until I couldn't stand it for another second. Everything inside of me burst into fragments, shattering into even smaller pieces until I wasn't even sure if I existed anymore. I cried out and froze, seeing and hearing nothing. Only *feeling*.

He pressed his tongue against my clit, prolonging the orgasm even more, and cupped my butt. "Fuck, Carrie," he groaned.

Then he drove inside me—hard and fast. Having him inside me felt so fabulous I wondered for a second if I was dreaming. But then he thrust back into me, and I snapped back into reality. And Finn in real life was *so* much better than a fantasy.

I dropped my head to the mattress when he withdrew almost all the way, closing my eyes tight and holding my breath in anticipation. When he was almost all the way out, he thrust back inside of me, then repeated the motion until I was whimpering and moaning his name.

He picked up the tempo, and tears stung my eyes. The amount of pleasure he was bringing down on me was actually making me cry. Pleasure so strong I couldn't even freaking handle it without whimpering into the mattress as he barreled into me again and again without restraint. He withdrew, flipped me over on to my back, and drove inside me again. When he changed his angle, going even deeper, I screamed.

Actually *screamed*.

My toes curled and I clenched down on him, my walls squeezing. He groaned and pumped faster, his face lost in the rapture of the moment. When he thrust inside me again, he went spiraling over the edge and collapsed over me, keeping his weight on his elbows.

Once we regained control of our breathing, he rolled to the side and dragged me with him. I clung to him and rested my head on his chest, right over the spot where there wasn't a tattoo. It was on the tip of my tongue to ask him if he had plans for that spot, but I realized I couldn't form a coherent word.

So I smiled instead.

"That was a nice way to forget about the stress, huh?" he asked, his lips twitching. He played with a piece of my hair, gently tugging on it. It made me shiver. "And here I was going to suggest surfing as a good method of forgetting about shit."

I took a deep breath, hoping when I opened my mouth that something besides an unintelligible grunt came out. "We can do that in the morning. I have a late class," I said, my heart finally settling back into a normal rhythm. And, lo and behold, I could talk. "But as far as this particular method of distraction goes? I plan on doing it again and again and again until this weekend…"

"Uh-huh. I see, I see." He nodded and pursed his lips seriously, as if we were discussing world politics. "But then what? We just stop?"

"No, then we find out what's next." I leaned up and kissed him softly. "And we deal with it."

But I really wanted to know what *it* was.

Sooner rather than later.

CHAPTER FOUR

Finn

"Let's go do something fun," I said, my hand on her lower back. She'd just finished studying, and we'd been sitting in silence ever since. I needed to make her stop thinking about what we'd be going through. "What's something you've always wanted to do but never did?"

"Skydive?"

I flinched. "I can't pull that together on short notice."

"Bungee jumping?"

I laughed uneasily. "Do you have a fucking death wish? Jesus."

She rolled her eyes. "Nope. I just like the rush."

"Yeah, well, tone it down a notch. How about roller-skating? Or ice-skating? Or what about—"

"Rock climbing." She sat up straight, her eyes lighting up. "I've always wanted to rock climb."

"Seriously?"

"Seriously." She nodded enthusiastically. I hadn't seen her this excited since the time I told her I'd teach her how to surf. "Do you know how?"

"I used to do it as a kid. Back when my dad still worked here."

"Were you good?"

I tugged on my hair. "My mom had tons of videos of me doing it. I found them the last time I went through the boxes in our attic. I guess I was okay."

"Your mom recorded you?" She smiled and squeezed my hand. "That's so cute."

I nodded. "She was that kind of mom. She came to everything with that damn camera in her hand."

Without even realizing it, I grinned, remembering how much it used to embarrass me. Now, I'd give anything to have her on the sidelines, watching me through a lens and cheering me on. She'd died of cancer when I was sixteen. I hadn't been the same since.

Carrie squeezed my hand again, then dropped a kiss on my jaw. "Let's go do it. Your mom would like to see you back up on a wall, I bet."

She probably would. She'd always said she loved seeing me out there, climbing higher and higher as if I already owned the world. I used to think I did back then. I stood up and helped her stand. "All right. But it's been years, so I'm probably not going to be the best teacher."

"I don't care." She laughed and headed for the door, her step already lighter. She picked up her helmet and grinned at me, her blue eyes dancing with excitement. "It'll be fun. Just you and me and the memory of your mom. Maybe I'll even take a video, love."

I swallowed hard and picked up my phone. I shot a quick text to her dad, then shoved it into my pocket. He'd been a little quiet lately. Must be busy working.

But still. Weird.

"Yeah. Fun." I grabbed my motorcycle keys and my helmet. "So, we'll need to make sure the place supplies the helmets, elbow guards, and knee pads."

"Or we could just climb." She opened the door. "I'll hardly be going that high. I think I'll be all right without all the padding."

I considered this, but shook my head. "I have a feeling they require safety equipment."

"Finn." She sighed. "Don't be my dad. You know I have enough of that in my life. I've already surfed and rode a bike. What's a little harmless rock climbing?"

She had a point, but it was my job to keep her safe. I sighed and followed her down the stairs. "Be that as it may, you will still need protection. They won't let you climb up without it. You might want to be free and wild, but they'll disagree."

"If they do, I'll listen to them." She pulled her helmet down over her head. "Just not you."

"Wow." I frowned at her. "I love you, too," I muttered.

She snorted. "Stop pouting. I'll probably fall off as soon as I get off the ground, which is why they make you wear a harness thingy," she said, motioning for me to get on the bike. "I wouldn't worry about me going too high up."

"Not helping my confidence here." I revved the bike. "Climb on, Ginger."

"Later, maybe," she replied, climbing onto the bike and holding tight. She yelled over the engine of my Harley. "But first, we rock climb!"

I laughed, loving her enthusiasm. She always dived in to new things with wide-open arms, never showing a hint of fear. Hell, she'd even done that with me. Just kind of opened up and accepted me for what I was. That never ceased to amaze me.

The whole ride to the closest rock climbing gym—a quick Google search had showed me the one I used to go to still existed—she held on to me, leaning when I leaned, resting while I rested. She had the bike thing down more perfectly than some drivers did. Maybe some day I'd teach her how to drive this thing. I bet she'd like that.

I parked and we went inside. It took all of five minutes for us to pay, then we were strapped into the harnesses and standing in front of a wall that looked a lot higher than I remembered.

"Okay, you put one foot on and kind of push up like this." I did what I described and climbed up a little unsteadily, almost catching myself off guard. Hell, it had been a long time for me. "But make sure to hold on tight with your hands while spreading them—but not too far. You don't want to throw off the balance."

She watched me, her brow furrowed, then did as I said. She set one foot up high, tested her weight, but then righted herself. She lifted her other foot, her brow furrowed with concentration. "Like this?"

"Yep." I climbed up a little higher again. "Do it again."

She did it, much more steadily this time. "It's almost rope climbing, only you're stepping instead of wrapping yourself around something."

"Except the wall," I said dryly.

"Well, duh," she said, rolling her eyes. "Obviously."

I stretched my arms and took another step higher. "Attitude, Ginger. Attitude."

"Now you're just showing off." She followed me, going a lot faster this time. I wanted to grab her and steady her when she wobbled, but I clenched my fists and let her do it for herself. She needed this. "Look, that was pretty good, huh?"

"Yeah, it was." I grinned at her. "Watch this."

I climbed double the length that I'd been doing, stretching my muscles as far as they could go without falling off the damn wall. She laughed, her eyes shining. "I can do that, too."

I side-eyed her. "You think?"

"Dude." She pursed her lips and looked to the top of the wall. "What is the worst that can happen? I fall and the harness catches me? Somehow I think I'll survive."

I shook my head. "Fine. It's your ass, not mine."

Technically, it was mine, too. I was supposed to be protecting her, not taking her rock climbing, but whatever. The girl needed to live, for fuck's sake.

She'd spent her whole life being watched by men like me not letting her step out of line for even a second. Now she was able to do so. I might be watching her, but I'd be damned if I suffocated her like her father.

We spent the next half hour climbing higher and higher, then we practiced climbing down. She slipped and fell more times than I could count—fine, it was seven—before we finally called it quits. I let her be the one to decide when she'd had enough.

She stood at the bottom of the wall after her last fall, snapping pictures and a few videos with her phone. Her laugh rang loud and clear as I descended to join her. She was so fucking bright and happy. She really was the sun to me.

The only thing that brought true brightness to my world.

I pushed back off the wall, landing nimbly on my feet, and she clapped, her phone held in her hand. "I got the perfect shot of that." She walked over and held out her phone. "And now I have a wallpaper for my phone, too. Nice, huh?"

It was of me in midair, about to land. It was a pretty cool shot. "Good one."

"Thanks. But I'm hungry now," she said, tucking her phone away. "You ready for some burgers or something?"

"McDonald's or Islands?" I asked, unclicking my harness and grabbing her hand. "You can pick tonight."

After we cleaned up and squared off with the workers, we walked toward my bike, her under my arm. "I think I'm gonna have to go Islands."

I grinned. "Did I convert you?"

"Maybe." She pointed a finger at me and glared, but the effect was ruined by how damn happy she looked. "But I'll forever be a McDonald's girl, too."

I shrugged. "Whatever you say, Ginger. Whatever you say."

CHAPTER FIVE

Finn

The next morning I woke up to Carrie climbing on top of me, kissing me until I forgot what the hell color the sky was. Her hands moved all over me, slowly waking me up, and by the time we were finished with each other, I was exhausted and naked and sweaty. I looked over at her and grinned at the smug smile on her face.

"More distraction, I see." I tapped her nose. "You look awfully proud of yourself."

"That's probably because I'm feeling pretty darn proud of myself."

She rolled over on her side, folded her hands under her cheek, and smiled at me. Something in her eyes pulled at me. Told me that beneath the smile and laughter was fear. Lots of fear.

But how could she manage to look so sad while still looking so damn happy?

"Get over here," I said.

When I opened my arms, she rolled into them and closed her arms around me. I held her for a few minutes, enjoying the closeness, not needing to talk. It was nice having a person with you where you didn't feel the need to blabber on and on just to fill the silence. As I was beginning to wonder if she fell asleep, she sighed and squirmed.

I played with her hair. I was beginning to think I had a hair fetish when it came to her. I couldn't stop myself from doing it. "Hey, you want to go out on a date tonight? Are you all caught up on your homework and shit?"

She rested her chin on me. "A date? Like, dresses and suits and a fancy restaurant?"

I hadn't been thinking of wearing a suit, no. I'd been thinking burgers or something along those lines. But I guess that's what a girl like Carrie expected when the word *date* came up. She'd grown up in the lap of luxury after all. If she wanted to wear a dress and go to some French restaurant I couldn't even pronounce, then so be it. I could certainly afford it.

I smiled at her. "Yeah. We can go to that French place on Pico. The one with the swans."

She brightened up, her smile wide. "Oh my God, yes! I've been wanting to go there for a while."

"Great," I said, smiling, even though I didn't feel like smiling.

"But I have to admit, I'm surprised to hear you suggest it. You're more of a burger-and-shake kind of guy," she said, her voice cheerful.

"And you're not?"

Her mouth twitched. "I'm not a guy."

"And thank fucking God for that." I tapped her nose with my finger. "But you know what I mean."

"I like them both," she said, lifting a shoulder in a tiny shrug. "A little bit of variety never hurt anyone."

Having her get all excited about a date in an expensive restaurant made me feel anxious and wound up. Shaking off the weird feeling creeping up my spine, I asked, "Do you still want to go surfing?"

"I do." She rested her chin on my chest. "It looks cloudy out, so there might be some awesome waves."

I tucked her red hair behind her ear and forced a smile. "All right. Want to eat before or after?"

"After." She got out of bed and looked over her shoulder at me. "But make sure you get some coffee in your system. I don't want to deal with cranky Finn."

I laughed and rolled out of bed. "*Cranky* Finn?"

"Mmhm." She reached into her bag and pulled out her red bikini. "He's miserable without coffee in him. A real jerk."

I came up behind her and nuzzled her neck. The feel of her skin on mine almost made me say the hell with surfing…but if she wanted to surf—then she'd get it. "Don't worry. I'll go make some now." As I headed bare-assed naked into the kitchen, I called out, "I'm surprised you remembered your suit."

"I thought we might end up going." She peeked over her shoulder at me as she stepped into the bottoms. "But we'll need to get my board from my dorm."

"You can leave it here if you want," I said, slipping a K-cup into the Keurig. "I don't mind."

"Really?" She stood up straight, wearing nothing but her tiny red bikini bottoms. Fuck, if she would let me, I'd snap a picture and make *that* my wallpaper. "Okay, sure."

"You look surprised," I said, raising a brow at her. "Why?"

She picked up the bikini top and turned almost as red as it was. "I always thought guys were weird with girls leaving their stuff at their places. They get all paranoid she's trying to stake a claim or something."

"Maybe some guys are, but I'm not one of those guys." I pulled two mugs out of the cabinet and headed back into the bedroom portion of my apartment. The light blue comforter was halfway off the bed, thanks to our morning sex. I straightened it, then pulled it up over our pillows. "Besides, the guys who don't want their girls' stuff at their places are the ones with something to hide. I don't have any more secrets."

She nibbled on her lower lip as she did up her bikini top, tying it in front of her breasts before sliding it up over her neck. "I know that. But you had a pretty big secret before that."

"You mean the fact that I was your father's secret bodyguard sent to watch over you?" I snorted. "That's nothing. What you really should know about me is this: I snore when I'm drunk."

She smacked me playfully. "Don't make me hurt you…and in that case? Maybe I'll need to leave some earplugs here."

"You can leave them right next to the bed." I hauled her into my arms, liking the idea of her leaving her shit here more and more. "You can leave some shirts and stuff, too, if you want. In case you ever need a quick change. Maybe a few of those books with abs on it that you like to read when you're not busy reading for school."

She blinked up at me. "Okay."

"Why are you looking at me like that *again*?" I flexed my fingers on her hips, not sure what the confused stare she wore meant. Did she not like the idea of leaving stuff here? Maybe I was moving too fast for her. Shit if I knew. "It's just clothes, Ginger. It's not a big deal. You have tons of them—just leave a few here instead of leaving them in a box that says 'free: take one' on the front."

She laughed and pushed out of my arms. "I *know*. Now shut up."

"Yes, ma'am." I tied my swim trunks and headed back toward the bathroom to brush my teeth. "Let me text your dad real quick. I've probably got like twenty texts from him already."

She rolled her eyes. "Remind me to tell you about Italy."

"Oh, that sounds…" I picked up my phone and swiped my finger across it. There wasn't a single message from him. Not a single one. That *never* happened. "What the fuck?"

She came up behind me and rested her hands on my shoulders, peeking around me to check my phone. "What? What's wrong?"

"He didn't text me." I opened his messages, scanning the time of the last text I'd gotten. "Shit. He hasn't texted me since yesterday."

"Is that different than usual?"

"Fuck yeah, it is." I swiped my finger up, showing her how many times he usually texted me. "He texts me like ten times a day, Ginger. But I've got nothing. *Nothing*."

She kissed my shoulder. "It's probably nothing to worry about. He's just busy, I bet. He called me yesterday at lunch and sounded fine. He wanted to let me know he might be a little bit quiet because of his schedule."

I relaxed a little bit, but it didn't feel right. Something was off, and I'd learned long ago to listen to my gut. If it said something was wrong, something was fucking wrong. "Yeah. Sure."

She let go of me. "Now go get ready. I want to get out in the ocean."

I headed for the bathroom, my phone still in my hand. As I brushed my teeth, I jotted off a quick text to Senator Wallington. *Carrie's okay. All is well.*

Within a minute I had a reply. *Thank you.*

That was it. A thank you. There was nothing wrong with the text, per se. But it wasn't right, damn it. I shook off the feeling that was bugging the fuck out of me, and focused on the date I'd promised Carrie. She had enough to stress about, what with that weird phone call I'd gotten that neither of us could make any sense out of, so I didn't need to go obsessing about the tone of a text message like some pansy-assed little girl.

I leaned against the door, my eyes on my reflection. The nagging sensation that something was wrong wouldn't let go. On top of that, I figured out what was bugging me from when we'd talked about our date.

I stared at myself, all tattoos, dog tags, muscles, swim trunks and five-o-clock shadow—it hit me. The problem with her wanting a fancy date with flowers and dresses and jewelry and valet parking was *I* wasn't fancy.

I could put on an expensive suit and pretend.

I could afford to be that guy, money-wise.

But underneath the suit and the charming smile, I was the tatted-up Marine that had no place dating the daughter of a prospective President of the United States of America. She was supposed to be with a trust fund baby. One who had money and wealth and recognition.

Me? I *so* wasn't that guy.

I never would be.

CHAPTER SIX

Carrie

The waves were strong, but not so much that I had to worry about being taken under. Thank God. I'd already been there once before, right after I found out Finn was working for my father, and I had no desire to be there again.

I looked over at him, and he was watching me, his warm blue eyes shining. His light brown hair looked almost blond in the sunlight, and his wetsuit clung to his muscles like a second skin. And I knew under that suit was a perfect body with an even more perfect heart underneath of it. He smiled at me, but I could tell it was strained.

He was upset about Dad not texting him, and I was, too. Even though I played it off like it was no big deal, it did sound bad. I called him while Finn was in the bathroom, and he hadn't answered. That freaked me out.

Almost as much as the call Finn had gotten from his commanding officer.

And it was killing me to act like it wasn't killing me.

"Hey, back at my place you told me to remind you about a story," he said, his tone light and teasing. It didn't fool me, though. He was stressed—and so was I. "What happened in Italy?"

My cheeks heated, and I looked over my shoulder. Why had I told him I'd tell him about that? Ugh. "Well, for me to explain, I have to tell another story first. You might already know it. Did you hear about what happened in Nevada when I was ten?"

Finn's brow creased. "No. My dad wasn't there yet. I was still in California. My mom was still alive…" He trailed off, his eyes focused on a past I couldn't see. "At that point in my life, I was a carefree surfer boy who thought he was invincible. My dad worked on a high-security detail for the governor, and my mom was healthy as a horse."

I nodded, wanting to probe more about what his life had been like before his mother died, but knowing now was not the time. He wanted his story, so I would give it to him. "There's a reason my dad is as crazy as he is. Back then, he wasn't so insistent we have security on us twenty-four/seven. I had freedom and there were actually times when I was on my own. We were free."

"You didn't have someone on you constantly?"

I shook my head. "Nope. In fact, Mom and I got bored while Dad was campaigning, so we decided to go shopping at the local mall to pass some time. We didn't bring anyone with us."

"I think I see where this is going," he said dryly. "You got lost and he panicked?"

I shook my head. "Nope. We got abducted."

"W-What?" he said, sitting up straight. "Are you fucking kidding me?"

"I wish." I sighed and looked over my shoulder. I hated talking about it. It had been a nightmare. "The guy was a complete idiot, so they found us pretty quickly, but my dad got really shaken up about it. We all did. And ever since then, he's been different. Controlling."

He sighed. "I almost get it now. If something happened to you on my watch, I'd probably go insane, too."

"Even though we were the ones who were abducted, I think he's the one who had the major post-traumatic stress issues. Mom and me?" I shrugged and stared out at the ocean before turning to Finn. "We moved on, but with the security that Dad insists follow us *everywhere*. And it's stayed that way ever since."

Finn nodded, his hands tight on his board. "So that's why he makes me follow you around out here."

"Yeah." I watched a fairly large wave form in the distance, rolling slowly toward us. I loved the way the waves did that—started small but slowly built up height before crashing to the sand. I could sit here all day and watch Mother Nature do her worst. "And in Italy, I escaped the watchmen."

Finn flinched. "Please tell me you weren't kidnapped."

"I wasn't." I smiled at him. "But I didn't answer my dad's texts and he freaked the hell out. I mean, catastrophic panic."

Finn tapped his fingers on his board, playing a tune I didn't recognize. "I would've been away then. I missed the show."

"You're lucky. I hear it was quite ugly." I sighed and tore my eyes from the water, looking back at my other favorite sight—otherwise known as Finn.

"Where did you go? In Italy?"

"I wanted to flirt with that guy I told you about when we first met. The Italian guy I mentioned. Remember him?"

His brows slammed down. "I do. But do I want to hear anything else?"

He was glowering at me now, but at least he looked more alive than he had for a while. Ever since he asked me on a date he'd been acting weird. Brooding, almost. I could tell something was bothering him, but I had no idea what it was or if it was even related to our date later tonight.

"Oh, don't look at me like that. I never even got close to him. My dad's guards found me and *took care* of it," I said, lifting my hands and doing air quotes. "But for those thirty minutes when no one knew where I was? Dad texted me every single second, I kid you not. I'd ignored him because I knew he was being his normal spaztastic self, and I told him as much. But after that, he promised to only text me twenty million times if it was an emergency."

Finn pressed his lips together. "So you're telling me this to make sure I don't panic like him, or what?"

"Pretty much." I reached out and caught his hand, squeezing it tight. "It'll be okay. You'll see."

"I know." He lifted my hand and kissed my fingers, making my stomach clench. "With you at my side, how could it not be?"

My heart melted at that sentence. Combined with the way he looked at me—his eyes soft and his lips even softer—I wasn't sure I had the muscle power to surf right now.

"You catch the first wave," I said, my voice practically a whisper. I cleared my throat and tipped my head toward the approaching wave. "It looks pretty big."

He nodded once. "And you'll wait till I come back to catch another one."

"Yeah, yeah." I waved a hand at him impatiently. "I remember the rules, master of the sea."

He looked over his shoulder, more than likely calculating the time it would take for his ride to arrive. He had a few seconds at most. He shot me a look and started paddling forward, his back muscles bunching and rolling flawlessly. "You can give me all the attitude you want, but I almost lost you once—I won't do it again."

"I know," I called out, splashing water at him. The drops barely reached him. "Now go before you're too late."

He grinned and flawlessly caught the wave, riding it to shore like the pro he was. He sliced in and out, doing moves I didn't even know the names of, never once tipping off balance. He was mesmerizing and beautiful to watch out here.

Well, *anywhere*. But especially on the water.

I watched him with awe, quite certain I'd never get to that level of skill, but I was okay with that. I just liked coming out here, hanging out in the water and enjoying the time with Finn. For the most part, we were left alone. There were a few surfers out this morning, but it was much emptier than on a weekend.

A blond man prepared to catch the next wave a few hundred feet over, and past him a woman with black hair bobbed in the water. It was a perfect, peaceful morning.

But I felt anything but peaceful.

Finn swam back to my side and I forced a bright smile. If it was the last thing I did, I would hide my anxiety from him. He didn't need my baggage sinking him down to the bottom of the Pacific. "That was a good one."

He climbed back on his black board and shook his hair like a wet dog, spraying me. "It was. Next one's yours, though."

"As long as it's little enough to pass your test," I added, unable to resist teasing him. Truth be told, I liked how protective he was. He loved me and he didn't want to lose me. I totally got that. "Right?"

"Right." He looked over his shoulder and trailed his fingers through the water absentmindedly. "Here comes a good one."

I paddled forward, watching the wave swell closer. "See ya on the flip side."

"Remember, if you go under, wait it out," he called, his voice tight.

I nodded as I paddled faster, ignoring the fear surging through me as the wave grew and grew. Apparently, that near drowning affected me more than I thought. I refused to let it conquer my enjoyment of the sport. Heck, people got limbs chewed off by sharks and went back out there. What was an almost drowning in comparison?

I struggled to my feet, wobbling a bit at first, but as I straightened my legs and stood, I gained my footing—and my confidence. As I rode the wave, holding my arms out for balance, I laughed from the sheer joy of the rush. I didn't attempt any fancy moves or anything—it took all my concentration just to stay upright.

But my head pounded and my heart raced, making me lightheaded. God, I'd become such an adrenaline junky since meeting Finn. I wanted to do all the things, and I wanted to do them now—with him at my side. Once my ride was over, I stood up and squeezed the excess moisture out of my hair.

I made my way back to Finn, a smile on my face the whole time. I'd missed this. Missed surfing, even though it had only been a week or two since we last came out. Maybe this weekend when Finn was gone, I would—

I stopped walking, a tingling sensation creeping up my spine. I had the weirdest feeling that someone was *watching* me, but when I looked over my shoulder, the beach was empty. The only people out and about were surfers, and none of them were paying any attention to me. I shook off the creepy sensation, forcing myself to keep walking.

It was all the uncertainty messing with my head, I'd bet. All the what ifs and Finn's own suspicions about my father's silence were screwing with me. Maybe reliving the time I'd been kidnapped contributed to my imagining someone watching me. That hadn't exactly been a walk in the park or a happy memory to retell.

All of this stressful crap was obviously combining in one tight ball in my head, making me think the shadows were chasing me. Making me think I was being watched, when the only one watching me was my bodyguard *slash* boyfriend.

I had enough to stress about. I needed to stop imagining new things. The whole way back to Finn, I thought about what life would be like after this year was up.

I was terrified about what Dad would do when he found out Finn and I had fallen in love. He could totally flip out, or he could—unlikely, as it might be—accept it for what it was. Maybe he would be angry, but he'd get over it with time. Or maybe we would never be welcome in his house again.

He *could* be quite stubborn when he wanted to be. It's admittedly where I'd gotten my stubborn streak from. And I wouldn't put it past him to make it a point to show me how many different ways I'd disappointed him through lectures and maybe even a little bit of a disowning shame. But he wouldn't actually cut the ties with me all because I dared to fall in love.

At least I hoped he wouldn't.

It was a risk I was willing to take for Finn.

CHAPTER SEVEN

Finn

Later that night, I waited in the living room as Carrie finished getting ready in my bathroom for our date. Even though we were only going out to dinner, I was nervous for some stupid ass reason I couldn't quite put my finger on. It was our first real date, yeah, but I didn't think that's what was bothering me. I just felt...

I don't know. Different somehow.

As if I was pretending to be something I wasn't. *Again.*

I tugged on my collar. Jesus, I swore the thing was single-handedly attempting to choke the life out of me. I was also starting to think it might win. My palms were sweaty, and I was so hot I didn't think I was going to make it through the night in this damned contraption. Maybe I'd had more Cali Surfer Boy left over in my blood than I'd thought.

Or maybe I was going soft.

I flopped down on the couch, setting my legs on the coffee table. This dress-up date was probably a bad idea. I wasn't a fancy guy, even if she was a fancy girl.

I was just *me*.

Why did I feel like I needed to be this guy for her all of a sudden? Maybe it was because I was more than likely leaving, and I was having a panic attack of sorts, trying to be everything she could ever possibly want me to be. Or maybe part of me just now realized that no matter what she said or thought, she came from a world where tuxes and champagne were more common than beer and movie nights…and if we were going to be together, I had to be in that world, too.

If I had any chance in hell in getting her father to accept me, I had to change. I had to be respectful and honorable and dress like *this*.

Go on dates like *this*. Be like *this*. And I fucking hated it.

Thinking about all the ways Carrie and I could go wrong made me realize her father still hadn't texted me even once. My heart clenched and I picked up my phone, scanning through our messages. The last text he'd sent on his own had been the morning Carrie had woken up late for school.

I tightened my jaw and typed: *Carrie is home and taking it easy tonight.*

A whole minute passed with no reply. What. The. Fuck?

If he wasn't answering my texts, I didn't know what the hell to think. First the odd call from my commanding officer, and now I was being ignored by a man who had previously needed me to hold his hand all this time. These were *not* good things. I knew it—even if I had no clue what the hell was going on in my life lately.

The bathroom door opened, and I stood up, tugging on my suit jacket as I turned to face her. I was about to ask her if she'd heard from her father, but then I turned around, and she stole the words right off the tip of my tongue. She took my breath away with her beauty, and it would never cease to amaze me how much of an effect she had on me.

I'd told her to wear a dress because we were going out somewhere nice, and she'd pulled out all the stops. She wore a dark purple dress that I suspected might melt if I touched it, it looked that soft. It clung to her body perfectly, highlighting everything that made her…well, her.

She topped it off with her long, red hair cascading down her back, just enough makeup to bring out her gorgeous blue eyes I loved so much, and a pair of black heels that would be over my shoulders by the end of the night if I had anything to say about it.

I didn't know whether to drool, throw her on the bed and hide her from the world, or take her out for all to see. The old me would've hidden her. Kept her to myself selfishly. But the new me? The *me* I was trying to be for her?

Not so much.

"You look beautiful," I managed to say through my tight throat and the even tighter tie. "Really fucking beautiful."

She dipped her gaze over me, her eyes lighting up in that way that told me she liked what she saw. "Dude. You look *hot* all dressed up. Like, really hot. I never thought I'd prefer you in something besides a pair of board shorts and a bare chest, but *hel-lo.*"

I grinned, but my heart dropped to the pit of my stomach. I'd been right. This is what she wanted from me, even if she didn't know it yet. "If you like it, then you'll get it anytime you want."

"I'll take both versions of you, please," she said, grinning. She ran her hands over my shoulders, smoothing my jacket. "I never thought I'd see you in one of these. It's blowing my mind."

I forced a smile. "I wear them for work all the time, Ginger."

"I know." Her hands fell back to her sides and her smile faded. "Is something wrong? You seem…upset or something. Different."

That's because I feel different right now. I shook my head and continued smiling, wanting nothing more than a shot of some hard liquor right now. "No. Nothing's wrong. You ready to go?"

"Sure." She started to grab her helmet, but I tugged her away. "Fancy people don't ride motorcycles. They take limos."

Her eyes went wide. "Limos? Seriously?"

I tried to read the expression in her eyes, but I couldn't tell if she was pleased by my surprise. I knew she was trying to get away from the life of glamour and glitz, but I needed to prove to her, and maybe myself, that I could do this. That I could thrive in her world, even if I wasn't so sure I could.

I opened the door for her. "That's what you ride back home, right?"

"If we're going to some sort of event?" She walked past me, her grip on her purse firm. "Sure. All the time."

I closed the door behind us and locked it. "We're going to an event. A date. Kind of our first date, I guess."

"You didn't have to…" She trailed off and stopped walking halfway down the stairs. "Oh my God. Is that…?"

When she didn't finish, I cleared my throat. "The same type of car you use back home? Yes."

"Wow," she said, her voice strung tight.

She wasn't happy with my surprise. It only seemed to solidify my belief that I didn't belong in her world. I tugged on my hair and eyed her. "We can cancel this whole thing if you want. Take the bike and go to Islands or something."

She pressed her lips together. "It's fine. I'm fine. Come on."

Deep in the back of my mind, I wondered if she was trying to picture me sitting in a fancy restaurant and not meshing the Finn she knew with the Finn I needed to be. Maybe that's why she looked as if I was torturing her instead of taking her out.

I urged her along, using my hand pressed against her lower back to propel her along. The sooner we got this date over with and I made her happy, the better. Then we could come back home, shed our clothes, and maybe share a cold drink over some good old-fashioned American television. Maybe some football, if I could find a game.

Man. I couldn't wait for that.

The driver opened the back for us, and I helped her inside. After following her, I settled into my seat and reached for the stocked bar. I poured myself a hefty dose of whiskey. Thank God they had the good stuff in here.

I took a long draught and reclined in the seat. When I looked at Carrie, she was watching me with narrowed eyes. I froze with the glass pressed to my lips. "What?"

"Why are we even doing this? You look miserable."

That's because I am. But it wasn't her fault. It was my own. I'd done this to myself, and I would damn well suffer through it with a grin on my face. "I'm taking the woman I love out on a date. How could I be miserable?"

She eyed me. "I don't know, but something's off. What is it? Is it the suit?"

How could she read me so fucking well? "No. I'm fine, Ginger."

"Yeah. Okay."

I gritted my teeth. "Drop it. Kick back and enjoy the date, okay? Stop worrying about everything so damn much and relax."

Her eyes flashed at me. I'd gone and pissed her off now. "No, I'm not going to *relax*. Something's wrong and you're not telling me what it is," she insisted, her eyes flashing with determination. "Just tell me why you're being all pissy and we can fix it."

"Jesus, Carrie. We can't fix everything with a conversation," I snapped.

She blinked at me, her cheeks flushed with color. "You're being a jerk," she said, her voice soft. "I don't like it."

Immediately, shame rushed through me fast and hard and relentless. I was yelling at her when I was supposed to be showing her a good time. Being a good fucking boyfriend. I dragged a hand through my hair and forced a smile. "I'm sorry. That was mean. I'm just…tired and stressed out. Maybe I should have had another cup of coffee tonight."

"I don't believe you," she said, her voice small and hurt. "You're not being yourself right now, and it has nothing to do with coffee."

Something snapped inside me, and I replied without thinking. "You're damned right I'm not, because right now I'm realizing that this is the *me* I'm going to have to be from now on. I guess I hadn't really thought about it much, but now it's the only thing I can think about." I finished the last of the whiskey and grabbed the bottle for some more. I could feel her watching me the whole time. "I used to attend these damn balls and galas, but I stood in the shadows, where no one saw me. Now when I go? I'll be judged…and more than likely found lacking."

"Welcome to my world."

I slapped my hand on my knee. "I didn't know it would be mine, too. I didn't know…" I fought for the right words, but nothing came. "I didn't know, okay?"

She looked confused. Her nose wrinkled up and she looked at me as if she didn't even recognize me. "I didn't ask you to dress up for me or to stand in the spotlight. You don't even have to go with me when I go to those things. And I wouldn't make you do anything you didn't want to do, so don't act like I would."

That might be true for now. But what if we got married? Had kids? The likelihood of me being off in the background was slim to none. People would want to know all about me—all about us. I couldn't let her down.

"But don't you see?" I splayed my arms. "I'll do it for *you*, damn it. To make you happy."

"This isn't you. It's not us." She motioned at me, then the limo. "We don't dress like this, and we don't scream at each other in a limo. And it's not making me freaking happy."

"But you *want* it to be us." I took a long drink, welcoming the burning sensation, and pointed my glass at her. "You do. Admit it."

"What?" She paled, but her curled hands twitched in her lap as if she was considering hitting me. I deserved it. "Why would you say that? I've never—"

"I asked you on a date, and you got all excited about fancy dresses and limos and all that shit. You know where I wanted to go? Islands. Burgers and shakes. And as you so aptly pointed out—I like them. I'm that kind of guy."

"And I *like* that guy. Actually, I love him," she said, her eyes narrow on me. "But I'll be honest. This guy?" She gestured toward me and the bar. "I don't like him very much."

I sat up straight and finished my drink, then set it down a little too hard. Maybe I'd had too much too fast. "Yeah, well, it's the guy you're going to be stuck with, so get used to it. I'd have been just as happy eating at a burger joint."

"So we should've gone there," she snapped. I knew she was angry with me now. Knew I'd gone and ruined everything. Hurt her. But I couldn't seem to stop myself from lashing out at her. "You don't have to take me out to an expensive restaurant to make me happy. *God.* You should know that by now."

"Should I? I don't think so." I grabbed her hands, trying to entwine my fingers with hers, but she didn't uncurl her fists. "The girl I know surfs and goes to soup kitchens and isn't afraid to get dirty. The girl I know loves McDonald's and Islands and doesn't care about tuxes and dresses."

She snatched her hands back. "Yeah, and that's still *me*. Fancy dresses don't change what's underneath."

"That's exactly what I'm saying." I sighed and shut my eyes for a second, trying to find the right words to make her understand what I was thinking. When I opened them, she looked at me as if I'd killed her puppy in front of her and then served him up for dinner. "Look, I've been thinking, and—"

"Oh my God." She scooted into the corner of the limo, her lower lip quivering. "Are you...are you breaking up with me? Already?"

My mind whirled at that. "What? *No.*"

She took a shaky breath. "You scared the heck out of me. Never start a fight and then say, '*I've been thinking*' ever again." She smacked my arm hard, then did it again even harder. "Got it, *love*? And also? Don't take me on dates you're going to hate. That's not my idea of a fun time, for future reference."

"Fine. But tell me one thing, *Ginger*," I said, emphasizing the nickname in the same sarcastic way she'd done to me. "Why can't you admit you fucking wanted this date and stop acting like you don't? Why can't you admit you want suits and jewelry and limos? Why can't you admit who you are?"

She threw her hands up. "Okay, maybe I did want it for *one* night. Jeez, is that so bad? Does that warrant you yelling at me and acting like an alcoholic because you're forced to go out with me?"

"Are you fucking kidding me?" I looked out the window, trying to regain the calm I'd lost the second we'd started arguing. I'd been trying to tell her I had to change and would—but that it wasn't easy for me. And now we were in each other's faces screaming about shit that didn't matter. "I had two drinks. Two. Drinks."

"In three seconds," she snapped. "Why can't *you* admit *that*?"

I snorted. "When you're old enough to drink, you can lecture me about my drinking habits. Until then? Not so much. You're barely more than a baby as it is. You can grow the fuck up before you judge me."

She stiffened. "Excuse me?"

I swallowed hard, realizing I was being a complete ass. I was a failure and I was only making it worse with every word I said. How had we gotten here, and how the hell did we get out of this train wreck of a night? "Shit. This is getting out of hand. Maybe we should stop talking now."

"Yeah. Maybe we should. And maybe this whole date thing was a horrible idea," she agreed, her voice shaking. She jammed her finger into the button for the intercom, speaking to the driver directly and ignoring me. "Change of plans. Take me to the dorms at the University of—"

I zoned out as she gave her instructions, my head making a hollow ocean sound. How many chances would I get before she said the hell with me and moved on? I swallowed the bile rising in my throat and tried to fix the fucking mess I'd made by opening my mouth in the first place. "Carrie, look. I'm sorry. I shouldn't—"

She shot me the death glare from hell. "Don't. I don't want to hear it. I'd storm off right now if you wouldn't follow me because you *have* to because it's your *job*. This is a fight, and we'll get through it. But right now? This date? We're done. We're *so* freaking done."

49

My heart lurched and I scrambled to grab her hands. She jerked out of my reach and gave me a look that froze me in my tracks. She'd never looked at me with such…disappointment. Not even when she'd found out who I really was.

I swallowed past the crippling guilt trying to kill me. "Please, don't go. We can go back home and talk. There's nothing we can't work through without—"

The limo stopped and she shot me a dark look. "Conversations don't fix *every*thing," she threw back in my face.

She opened the door and got out, and I scooted after her. "I didn't mean that. I didn't mean any of this. I was just trying to explain how I feel."

"Well, you suck at explaining feelings." She stopped walking and scowled at me. "Tonight you're not my boyfriend. You're my bodyguard. So watch me go inside so you know I made it home safe—and then leave me alone. It's your *job*, right?"

I bit my tongue from lashing out at her. I didn't want to keep fighting, damn it. I wanted to *fix* this. "Are you always going to throw that in my face every time we fight?"

Shit. I hadn't bitten hard enough.

"Yeah. Maybe. Or, at least, I will until I *grow up*."

She stormed off, and I watched her go, knowing I was a fucking idiot for taking what should have been a great night and turning it into an awful memory.

As if we didn't have enough of those already.

CHAPTER EIGHT

Carrie

I stomped my way upstairs and made it to my room in record time. I hadn't slept in this room since the night before Finn and I got back together, and I really didn't want to be here now. I don't know what had happened out there, but it had escalated really, *really* fast. Like, supersonic speed fast.

I unlocked the door and shut it behind me, breathing heavily. I squeezed my eyes shut, refusing to cry. Refusing to let this get to me. We had enough crap going on right now, and then we had to go and ruin what should have been a date night with anger and shouting. What was wrong with us that we couldn't gain some sort of equilibrium where there wasn't something *wrong* all the time?

I smacked the door behind me with my open palm so hard it made my hand sting and ache. "Goddamn it all to hell."

"Uh, Carrie?" Marie asked, her voice quiet. "You okay over there?"

I opened my eyes and quickly located her. She sat at the table with her books open. She had her long platinum blonde hair in a sloppy bun, and black glasses perched on her perfect nose that only brought out her bright eyes even more. The irony of Marie home studying while I was out with a guy struck home as it well should.

That's probably what I should have been doing instead of fighting with Finn.

"Not really," I managed to say before I broke down and burst into tears. I quickly covered my face, trying to hide myself from her and the world. I didn't do this. Didn't cry in front of people. What had happened to me lately? "Oh my God. I'm so sorry."

"Shh," Marie said. I heard a shuffling sound and then her arms were around me. "Don't apologize. Just cry if you need to."

I took a gulping breath and sobbed into her shoulder, holding on to her as if she was the only thing keeping me afloat in the middle of the ocean. This whole situation was ridiculous, because we weren't even close, really, and yet I was crying all over her. By the time I finished, she was soaked and I was embarrassed more than words could say.

I pulled back and she hugged me tighter, not letting me go. "Give it another second. You might not be done yet."

I swiped my hands under my eyes and laughed nervously, feeling like a complete idiot. "I'm good."

"Okay." Marie let go of me and backed up a few steps, her lips pursed as she studied me through her glasses. "Now tell me what happened."

"I…well…" I broke off, not sure where to start or what to say. Or how much of it to say. "I got in a fight with my boyfriend."

"Boyfriend?" Her eyes narrowed. "Who is he?"

"No one you know. He doesn't go here." I waved a hand. "It's not important. He might be leaving soon, and we tried to have a romantic night, but we got in a fight."

"Where's he going?"

I swallowed hard. Call me crazy, but I wasn't ready to trust her with all my juicy secrets. We barely talked aside from the pleasantries most roommates shared such as *"I'll be out late tonight"* or *"I'm bringing a guy home."*

I met her eyes. "His work might be sending him away."

"Oh, that sucks." She nodded. "I dated a guy once who was a drummer in a band. It was right when we moved out here for school. He was never around, and when he was, all he wanted was sex. We never even talked, really. It took me a little while to realize I was nothing but a convenience for him when he was in town. He probably had one of me in every city his band played."

Marie pressed her lips together, looking angry at the memory. I reached out and squeezed her hand reassuringly. "He sounds like a real jerk."

"He was." Marie gave me a small smile. "Is that how your guy is?"

"No. He's…he's great," I said, my voice breaking. "That's why I have no idea what the heck happened tonight. One second he was fine, and the next he was yelling and being nasty. I've never seen him like that."

Marie nodded. "Do you think he's stressed out about maybe leaving? Stress can cause men to act like weirdos. One time my dad was acting like a jerk, and we had no idea why. Turned out, he had learned he had cancer and was processing it all. And one of the ways he did it was by ranting at the whole world."

I swallowed hard. It hadn't occurred to me until now, but Finn and Marie had both lost a parent at the same age. "God, that's awful. I'm so sorry."

"Yeah, it sucks," she said softly, her eyes sad despite her words. "But thanks."

I hugged her, feeling like an idiot. All this time I'd been judging her as vapid and empty, and here she was making me feel better. Sharing life stories with me. I hadn't treated her fairly, but I made a vow to stop doing it. "I'm sorry I've been so quiet with you. I…I'm not used to this kind of life. I'm not good at this."

Marie grinned. "You mean like how you didn't want to bathe the first week because people might see you in the communal shower?"

I facepalmed myself. "You noticed?"

"It was pretty hard to miss. You were hand bathing for a while."

"Yeah. It was pretty pathetic."

"Pretty much," she teased, her eyes sparkling again. "But anyway, about your man…do you think that's what this was about? Him taking out his stress on you?"

I straightened my back. "Now that you mention it, that's probably what this was. He's nervous and he lashed out at me. That's what he was trying to talk to me about. I'm such an idiot."

"It's not your fault. Guys are weird," Marie said, patting my back. "How are we supposed to understand how their brains work?"

"I have to go find him." I grabbed the knob, but froze with my hand on it. "Hey, thank you. I'm sorry I cried all over you. I owe you a shirt."

Marie grinned. "It's okay. It was kind of nice to be the one comforting someone else for once. I'm usually the one who's a mess." Marie met my eyes. "Besides, I picked one up from the lobby earlier. Thanks for the donation."

I froze. "You know?"

"Well, I did see it laying out on the bed earlier, and then it was in that mysterious donation box." She shrugged. "It wasn't hard to figure out. But don't worry. Your secret is safe with me."

"Thank you." I hesitated. "You can have first pick if you want."

She laughed. "I might agree to that."

"Okay." I still didn't leave. Instead, I looked at her again, trying to see past the smile and glasses. Maybe it was time to try being friends with a girl for once. I hadn't really wanted to try again, after all the girls I grew up with turned out to be major bitches. But maybe it was time to grow up a bit, like Finn said. "Hey, want to go get coffee sometime? Maybe talk some more?"

Her cheeks flushed and she wrapped her arms around herself. "I'd like that. Now go get him…whoever he is."

Maybe I'd tell her tomorrow, but tonight I had to go get my man.

I closed the door behind me and rushed down the stairs, passing a surprised-looking Cory without so much as a word. As I dialed the local cab company, I decided to see what I could do about getting a car ASAP. Calling a cab every other day was ridiculous.

"Yes, hello. I'd like a cab to get me at—" I broke off as soon as I saw him. Finn hadn't left. He sat on the bench outside my dorm room, his face in his hands. "Never mind."

I hung up on the cab company and slowly walked over to him. He looked so vulnerable.

He'd taken off his jacket and tossed it on the ground, and his tie hung loosely off his neck. My heart broke at the sight of him. When I stopped directly in front of him, I fisted my dress in my hands and tried to figure out what to say that wouldn't lead to another fight.

"You ready to talk without the fighting?"

His head snapped up and his bright blue eyes pinned me in place. He swallowed hard, his Adam's apple bobbing. "I'm sorry. So fucking sorry."

"I know." I sat down beside him and sighed. "I am, too."

He gave a harsh laugh. "You didn't do anything to be sorry for. I'm the one who took a simple conversation and turned it into this."

"I'm the one who got angry and didn't let you talk." I took a deep breath and rested my hand on his knee. "You're nervous, aren't you? That's what you wanted to talk about? What you were trying to say?"

He shook his head, his expression ironic. "Nervous? I'm fucking

54

terrified. I'm scared because your father isn't texting me, and I have to go talk to my C.O. I'm terrified because the one time that I try to do something nice for you, I fucked it up."

"It's okay. I get it."

"It's *not* fucking okay. That's not all I'm scared about." He dragged his hands down his face and looked at me, his eyes raw and open. "I'm scared your father is going to shove me out of your life when he finds out about us. That he's going to make you see I'm not good enough for you or your world. But most of all? I'm scared you'll realize it all on your own without him there to tell you."

I recoiled. That's not what I'd expected him to be scared of, for God's sake. He was supposed to be afraid of leaving and war and guns. Not something that would never, *ever* happen. "That's ridiculous."

"No, it's not. It's the fucking truth." He lifted his head. "How many presidents' daughters have you seen married to bikers, standing up there on the stage during the primaries, with their ink hanging out for all of America to see?"

All my life, I'd lived according to my father's plans. I'd missed my own graduation because we had to go out of town campaigning for the senatorial primaries. I'd given up everything for my father's agenda, but I *wouldn't* be giving up my Finn.

I pressed my lips together. "None. Now ask me how much I care about that?"

"You might not care now, but you will eventually." He gestured toward the moon, his entire body seeming tense and angry. And a little bit...defeated, maybe? "It's only a matter of time, but I have a plan. I'm going to—"

"Shut. Up."

He turned to me, his jaw squared off in that way he always did when he was determined to win a fight, but there would be no victory this time. "I know I said some mean things in our time together, but the truth is...you *are* younger than me. You don't know how cruel the world is. The first thing your father is going to say when he finds out about us— once he's done pounding me into the dirt, that is—is that I'm not good enough for you. And he'll be right. But I'm going to fix it."

"How many times do we have to go over this?" I asked through my teeth. "There's nothing to *fix*. We're not broken in the first place."

"I know you love me and you know I love you, too." He reached out and grabbed my hand, squeezing it tight. "But I can see how this is going to end, Ginger. I'll stay until you send me away, but it'll happen at one point *if* I don't take the necessary steps to avoid it."

I blinked away tears. "It sounds to me like you're just making excuses so you can walk away with a clear conscience."

He made a tortured sound and shook his head. "Hell no. Never."

"If you want to walk away…" I said, my voice breaking so badly I couldn't even finish the sentence. The mere thought of Finn leaving me was enough to break me.

He swiped away tears off my cheeks I hadn't even realized escaped, hugged me tight against his chest, and buried his face in my neck. "I don't want to lose you. I just say all this shit and ruin perfect nights because of my stupid fears, but I'm not scared anymore. I know what to do to make us work."

I curled my hands into his shirt. "We *already* work."

"Now, yeah. But once you graduate, it'll be different. We'll have to be different."

I wanted to fight him on this, but I knew no matter what I said, he wouldn't believe me. He was convinced I was my father's puppet who would break up with him if Daddy told me to. I'd have to prove him wrong. "What are you planning to do?"

"I'm going to change."

I narrowed my eyes, trying to make sense of his words. "I don't want you to change. Even if he doesn't like you, I won't care."

He rubbed my head almost absentmindedly. "It's the one conflict in our life I can see coming—and avoid. He's going to fire me. Hell, he could even sue me. It was in the contract that I couldn't touch you."

"He put that in there?" I asked, gripping my dress tight.

"Yeah."

I shook my head. My father was freaking ridiculous. "If he does, then we'll handle it together. Right?" I bit down on my lower lip. "Maybe you could do something else."

He pushed me away and squeezed my arms with a smile on his face. "Exactly. Like I said. *Change.*"

I hesitated, my heart picking up speed. This kind of *change* I could probably work with. "What are you going to do?"

"I can maybe change my MOS."

I blinked. "What's an MOS?"

"It stands for Military Occupational Specialty, but it's basically my position. My career in the Marines."

I nodded. "What would you change it to?"

"I'm not sure. Maybe I could go into active duty with the Marines. I bet that will look good on Election Day. Having a Marine up on the stage with him in Dress Blues. He can't complain about that, can he?" he asked me, his eyes on mine.

"No. Of course not." And just like that, down came my bubble. "But what about going back to school? Becoming a chef or a surf instructor? I don't know. *Something*." I shrugged. "Growing up, was there something you wanted to be?"

He blinked at me, a weird look on his face. "Um, I wanted to work on computers as a kid. You know, build them."

I perked up at that. Computers were safe. "Well, you could go to school for that."

"I could." He straightened up, blinking rapidly. "I don't even have to re-up when my time is up, if I don't want to. Or, I can become a commissioned officer and get a job in that field *through* the Marines." He snapped his fingers. "Ooh, yeah. That'll look really good on your father's campaign. An *officer* at his side."

"I don't care about his fucking campaign!" I shouted, my hands curled into tight balls. God, Dad had gotten to Finn, too. Without even trying. His reach was that freaking far. "I care about you. About *us*."

"But this *is* for us." He stood up and paced, his steps hurried and uneven. He stepped on his jacket and didn't even care. "We won't have to worry about what happens after he kills me—as long as he doesn't *actually* kill me, that is." He swung me into his arms and hugged me tight. "This obstacle between us? It's gone. I can be that guy."

The obstacle that didn't exist? Yeah. It was gone.

"I don't think you need to be any guy but you. I love you the way you are—tattoos and all."

He grinned down at me. "And I love you for that."

He kissed me hard, right in front of my dorm in the moonlight. I clung to him, gripping his dress shirt in my fists and pulling him closer. By the time he pulled back, I forgot all about what we were saying.

All I knew was Finn was smiling at me, and he looked happy.

I wasn't about to ruin it.

CHAPTER NINE

Finn

Wednesday night I waited on my bike outside Carrie's dorm. She had to study late with some friends from chemistry, so I told her I'd pick her up at eight. After our fight last night, I wasn't sure what to expect from her when she came outside. Would she still be mad at me, or had she really forgiven me for being an ass?

All I knew was I needed to get through the rest of the week, find out what my C.O. wanted from me, and then move on with my new life plan. I was more determined than ever to get through this year alive, get out of the Marines, and go back to college. Until Carrie, I hadn't wanted to do that. I had been perfectly content being a Marine.

But now? I wanted more. I wanted to be more.

For her *and* for me.

My phone buzzed, and I looked down at it with my heart racing. Had her father finally texted me on his own? I glanced down at it, but it was from Carrie. *Be down in two minutes.*

Okay. I shoved the phone into my pocket.

A few minutes later, she came out of her dorm, her usual bag over her shoulder and a gorgeous smile on her face, and she looked so damn happy. So much like my Carrie that she took my fucking breath away. I had no idea what I'd done to deserve her in my life, but I'd do it again and again if it meant I got to keep her forever.

I shook my thoughts and straightened my back, waiting for her to make her way over to me. When she was within reaching distance, I snatched her up and kissed her before she could say a word. I slipped my hand into her back pocket before carefully removing it.

Then, and only then, I let myself get lost in our kiss. I needed the affirmation that she was here and mine and happy, as pathetic as that might be. I pressed my mouth to hers, urging her to open to me. And when she did, I slipped my tongue between her lips and kissed her hungrily. As if I would never get enough of her sweet taste.

And I didn't think I ever would.

When I broke the kiss, she rested her hands on my shoulders and blinked up at me. "Wow. I should be late more often."

"That had nothing to do with you being late."

"Then what was it?"

"I wanted to kiss you, so I did." I shrugged, trying to play it off as if I wasn't going completely crazy right now. Because I abso-fuck-ing-lutely was. "Why were you late, anyway?"

"I was chatting with Marie." She glanced up at me. "We've been talking, and we have a lot more in common than I thought. We're getting coffee later this week."

I'd told her she should try talking to Marie some more. My Ginger wasn't the most open when it came to making friends—with reason. But Marie seemed a pretty safe bet. "That sounds fun."

"Yeah." She bit down on her lip. "I think she's homesick, and sometimes I get that way too, even with my crazy parents. She doesn't seem to have many people here, besides me. I'm lucky I have you."

She had a knack for finding the loneliest sucker and making her feel welcome with nothing more than a smile. It was one of the things I loved most about her. "She can have me too if you want."

She slapped my arm. "Haha, really funny."

"What? I was just trying to be supportive." I threw my arm around her. "But you know I'm kidding. I only have room for one college student in my life."

"I might take her to the soup kitchen with me this weekend while you're gone." She stole a quick peek at me. "If you don't mind, of course."

"Of course not," I said through the nervousness trying to strangle me. "But you have to leave with her, and not walk down any dark alleys."

60

"I'll leave before it's dark, I promise." She grabbed her helmet and tugged it on. When she was finished, I held out my hand for her bag. She handed it over and I slid it over my head, watching her the whole time.

I slipped my own helmet over my head and revved the engine, disgusted with myself. "You ready, Ginger?"

She glided on behind me and wrapped her body around mine. I'd never get sick of this feeling with her. This utter shiny happiness at her arms wrapped around me, her head on my shoulder. It never got old and I hoped it never would.

"Ready," she called out.

When we pulled up to my apartment building, I stopped the bike and took a deep breath. I'd made a move that she may or may not appreciate, and I was about to find out.

"I'm exhausted." She took off her helmet and started up the pathway toward the stairs. After yawning loudly, she added, "I need to do some more homework, then we're going to bed early. I didn't sleep well after you left last night."

I hadn't asked her to come home with me, and she hadn't suggested it. It still stung that after our first fight as a couple, we'd spent the night apart. "Yeah, me either."

"Next time, no matter the fight, we sleep together. Deal?"

"It's a promise," I said, leaning down to kiss her.

When she broke off the kiss, we walked hand in hand to the door. Halfway there, she looked over her shoulder, her brow furrowed. "Did you hear that?"

"Hear what?" I immediately stopped walking and pushed her behind me. I scanned the shadows for any sign of movement. "What did it sound like?"

"A footstep." She bit down on her lip. "Is someone watching us?"

I closed my eyes and listened. There wasn't a sound, not even a breath or a footstep. She was getting as paranoid as I was, because as far as I could tell, no one was there.

"I don't think anyone is there," I said, reaching behind me to squeeze her hand. "Maybe it was a raccoon or something."

"Yeah. Probably." She laughed uneasily. "I'm imagining things."

"Hey, better safe than sorry," I said, smiling at her. "If you ever think you see or hear something, definitely let me know. You might notice something I don't."

"I will." We reached the door and she waited for me to open it. When I didn't, she shot me a look. "Uh, are you going to open the door?"

My heart skipped a beat or two, and my palms grew sweaty. Was this a good idea? It was too late to go back now. I'd already made the steps toward this, and I wasn't one to back down. "*You* open it."

She looked at my empty hands first, then up at my face, her brow crinkled. "Okay? Give me your key."

I crossed my arms. "Why don't you use your own?"

"Maybe because I don't have one?"

"Check your back pocket," I said, my voice low. I really hoped she didn't freak out or throw the key back at me or tell me I was moving too fucking fast. When she just stared at me, her cheeks flushed, I tapped my foot. "Well? Go on. Check."

She slid her hand into the wrong pocket, then moved on to the right one. Hopefully it hadn't slipped out on the ride, or all this show was for nothing. When she pulled her hand out, the little gold key in her fingers, I held my breath and waited to see her reaction.

Slowly, her wide eyes rose from the key until her gaze collided with mine. "You gave me a key? To your place?"

"I did." I tugged on my hair and shifted on my feet. "If you don't want it, it's cool. I just thought it would be nice for you to be able to come over here whenever you wanted, even if I'm not here. You could come here and study, or sleep, or eat, or whatever you wanted even if I'm…"

…*not here.*

Yeah, I already said that.

I stopped talking and stared at my feet, because I was babbling like a fucking idiot. I didn't like acting like an idiot, although I'd been doing it way too much lately. Apparently, love and idiocy went hand in hand.

"Finn?"

I lifted my head and dropped my hand. "Yeah?"

"This is so…wow," she said softly. "Thank you."

I nodded, not sure what else to say. I wanted her in my home all the time, so I gave her a key. It was simple. "Go ahead and see if it works."

It did. I already tested it.

But at least it gave her something to do besides stare at me looking all happy and yet somehow sad. It's like she knew why I was really doing this. Even if I was gone, it would be like she was with me whenever she came here, and that meant something.

She slid the key into the lock and turned it, giving me a shaky smile when it opened. "It works."

"Good," I said, my voice gruff. "Go in, then."

She went inside and flipped on the light, stopping a few steps in. She stood in the middle of the living room area, her eyes on my closet. Not a big shocker there. After all, it became clear, quite quickly, that I'd cleared some space in my closet for her—complete with pink fucking hangers waiting for her shit.

Yeah. *Pink.*

"Did you…is that…?"

"For you?" I leaned against the door and crossed my ankles, trying to go for casual and unconcerned. "Yeah. Last time I checked, I didn't use pink. I know it doesn't go with your hair, but…" I shrugged, even though she wasn't looking at me. She was still staring at the closet. "I figured that would make the clothes stand out more, since you never wear it. Ya know?"

She walked up to the closet and ran her hands over the pink hangers, then touched my cammies before letting her hand drop to her side. "Are you sure?"

"Yeah, I'm sure." I crossed the room and came up behind her, resting my hands on her shoulders. I leaned down and kissed the top of her ginger head, breathing in the scent of the shampoo that I'd bought for her. "But are you?" I asked softly. "It's not like you're moving in or anything. It's just an open-door policy."

She nodded. "You know I'm not going anywhere, right?"

"I know you think that, and I know you want to believe it. And so do I." I wrapped my arms around her and hugged her close, more so to hide my face from her than anything. And I *really* didn't want to fight again. "But I've seen a lot more of the world than you have. Shit happens and life is hard. If I leave—"

She smacked me. "I'm not going to move on or forget you."

I flinched. "I know." Or, at least I knew she didn't *plan* on it. But plans changed, and so did people. Especially when they were separated. "That's not what I'm saying."

She tensed in my arms. "But you are. You're worried if you go on deployment I'll move on to another guy, aren't you? You don't trust me."

Oh, fuck. This was going to be another fight if I didn't fix it and fix it now. "Ginger…"

"No way. You're not getting off that easily."

My hands flexed on her, but she moved out of my arms. I missed her already. The softness in her blue eyes gave way to her icy look, and she put her hands on her hips. Oh yeah. I'd pissed her off. Damn it. "I trust you, Ginger."

"Don't *Ginger* me, mister." She poked a finger in my chest and I held my hands up in surrender. "Do you have such little faith in me that you think I would freaking leave you when you're off defending our country? *Really?*"

"You're not the one I don't have faith in," I said, squaring my jaw. "I'm worried I'll do something to fuck this up."

"How could *you* mess this up?"

Well, for starters I could *die*. But I didn't say that. She would only worry even more. I scrambled for some bullshit reason to give her, but came up a round short. So I shrugged and said nothing. She pushed me hard, back toward the bed, and I stumbled a little bit before I could catch my balance.

Was it somehow perverted that I liked her beating me up? Because I did.

She shoved me again. The back of my knees hit the bed, and I fell onto it, not even bothering to fight it. When I hit the mattress, she climbed on top of me and held my hands down. "I'm going to tell you this once and once only: I will not leave you. And if you leave, I will always be here waiting for you when you get back. Whether it's in a few days, a week, or a freaking year. I'll be *here*. I'll be *yours*."

Something inside of me gave way and broke. Maybe it was my doubt. Maybe it was something else. All I knew is what caused it. Her. "Fuck, I love you. So damn much it scares the shit out of me. I've never been scared of anything before. Guns. Surfing. War. But now I have the biggest fear of all—losing you."

"Finn…" she whispered, her voice breaking.

I slipped my hand behind her head and urged her down, kissing her the second her lips touched mine. Her fingers flexed on mine, and she moaned softly, straining to get closer to me. I slanted my head, deepening the kiss even more, and she wrapped her arms around me.

Man, I needed this in my life. Needed her lips on mine, her arms around me tight, her grip on my heart secure and complete. Without it, I'd be alive, and I'd be here, but I wouldn't be *me*. I wouldn't be *living*.

My hands moved down her back slowly until I cupped her ass, urging her even closer to my cock. She pressed down, a soft moan escaping her. She adjusted herself slightly so she straddled me, her legs tucked behind her, and she moved against me in a sensuous, perfect circular motion.

I lifted my hands higher, burying them in her hair and yanking her down harder. She whimpered into my mouth and curled her fingers into my pecs, moving her hips faster. She tugged on my shirt impatiently. I broke the kiss off long enough for her to yank it over my head, and then I rolled her beneath me.

Her legs closed around my waist, urging me closer, and my gut tightened. If she didn't stop making those little sounds, I'd be inside of her before she even came for me once. Slowly, I ran my hands over her breasts, lightly teasing her nipples. She arched into my hand, begging me for more without words, and I gave her what she wanted. Hell, I'd always give her what she wanted.

I was that much of a sap.

I cupped her, rolling my palms over her. The shirt had to go and so did the bra, so I stopped kissing her long enough to get her naked and grab a condom. As I stripped off her pants, I kissed a path down her thigh, over her knee, and nipped at her ankle. She cried out and pressed into the mattress, her breath coming in tiny bursts.

As I removed all my clothing, I watched her. I rolled the condom over my cock, never dropping my eyes from her. Her cheeks were flushed and her eyes were closed, and she trailed her hand lightly over her own stomach, a small moan escaping at the touch.

Holy fucking hell, she looked like a naughty angel brought to Earth. My angel…and I was never letting her go. Her father could kiss my ass. I was the man for her, and we both knew it. And wasn't that all that mattered? I'd spent all this time stressing about her father's reaction, when I should have been focusing on her.

I wouldn't make the mistake again.

I crawled up her body, leaving kisses and nips as I went, stopping only once I was at her hip. I rolled my tongue over her hipbone, my heart quickening when she cried out and scraped her nails across my shoulders. I loved the way she looked when she was turned on. All rosy cheeks and soft lips. All *mine*.

I flicked my tongue over her clit, my finger thrusting inside of her at the same time. She screamed and arched her hips; her breath coming out harsh and uneven. "God, *Finn*. Don't stop."

Oh, I wasn't planning on it. Not until she was a quivering mess.

I rolled my tongue over her, pressing a little harder, and moved my fingers in and out, building up the speed with each motion. When she tightened her legs on my head, a cry escaping her lips that sounded more like a breath than a word, I positioned myself between her legs. She scrambled to hold on to me, and I lifted her hips, driving inside of her with one smooth thrust.

"*Finn*," she cried, her nails raking down my back.

"Come for me again," I demanded in her ear, biting down on her shoulder and thrusting harder. "Let go for me."

She dug her nails into my back and held her breath, her pussy clenching down around my cock so hard that she almost pushed me out. When she came, her walls squeezing me until I couldn't fucking stand it anymore, I was right there with her, my hands gripping her as tight as I could as I soared into the sky.

When I came back down, she was running her fingers up and down my spine, kissing my shoulder over and over again. I knew, right then and there, that she'd meant every word she said. She'd be here waiting for me no matter what happened.

And it felt fucking amazing to finally, *truly* believe in that kind of love.

CHAPTER TEN

I looked up at Finn, trying to let my love shine out onto him, or light him up or something. It sounded stupid, in theory, but how many times have you looked at a couple and *known* they were completely in love just from the way they looked at one another?

If ever a girl looked at a guy that way, it had to be Finn and me.

I cupped his face like he always did to me, running my finger over his mouth. I could see why he liked doing it. It was sweet and made me feel closer to him. I repeated the gesture, rubbing the lip I had been kissing. "You okay?"

Because I couldn't live in a world where Finn wasn't okay.

"More than okay." He kissed me, light and teasing, then pulled back again. "But you have to study. I distracted you."

"I know." I smiled up at him. "But I guess I have some unpacking to do first, huh?"

"Lots."

He pushed off me, and I got dressed, watching him as he lounged back on the bed naked and completely okay with that. And so was I.

I could stare at him all night long, admiring the way the colors swirled over his hard muscles the whole time. His tattoos were perfect to me, but he seemed to think there was something wrong with them.

The fact that he thought he wasn't good enough for me and my father made my throat tighten. Would I ever be able to convince him I loved him exactly how he was, not as a version of what he could be? That I didn't want him to change at all?

Once I had on one of his green Hollister shirts and a pair of panties, I headed for the closet. His uniforms stared back at me, and I swear the things were alive. Like they were watching me. I was trying to act all confident about this whole possible deployment mess, but the truth was…I was scared, too.

He lifted on his elbows and watched me from the bed, his steamy eyes on me the whole time. I wanted nothing more in this world than to climb on top of him again and curl up in his arms. There was nothing in this world that his arms around me couldn't fix.

I picked up my bag and took out one of my shirts, hanging it up on the hanger. It meant a lot to me, him offering me this space in his life and his key. It was almost as if, when he was gone, I'd get to be here with him—even without him.

It didn't make much sense, yet it totally did.

And I liked the idea of sleeping in his bed when he wasn't here. Smelling him on his sheets. But how long would the scent of Finn linger if he left? A day? A month? I had no freaking clue, but I did know one thing: I needed to spend as much time as possible with him.

I put a shirt on the hanger and gathered by thoughts. My phone rang from beside Finn on the bed. He glanced down at it and his mouth tightened. He picked it up and held it out to me. "It's your father. He still isn't texting me like he used to, so be careful what you say. Try to get intel from him."

I nodded, crossed the room, and sat at his hip. After taking my phone out of his hand, I said, "Hey, Dad."

"Hello," Dad said, his voice clear and crisp. "Where are you?"

"You're up late." I checked the time, ignoring his question. It was almost midnight back home. Finn toyed with my hair, sending little shivers down my spine. "Shouldn't you be sleeping by now? And why have you been so quiet this week?"

"I told you I'd be busy," he said. "My turn for a question. Shouldn't *you* be in *your* room?"

I tensed, and so did Finn. He must've heard Dad's voice through the speaker. He dropped my hair and rolled off the bed. After grabbing his own phone, he swiped his finger across the screen. I raised my brows at him and he shook his head with a frown. He hadn't gotten any texts from my father asking where I was.

What was Dad up to, and what did it mean for us?

"Uh…" I forced myself to pay attention to Dad. "What makes you think I'm not in my room? Did you put a webcam up in it or something? I'm pretty sure I forbade cameras in my bedroom once I hit puberty."

He snorted. "Don't play coy with me, missy. I'm here, at your dorm, with your mother—and you're not here. Where are you?"

"Wait, *what*?" I leapt to my feet, my pulse racing and my knees trembling. "Why are you here in San Diego?"

Finn cursed under his breath and dialed someone. He grabbed his pants off the floor and stepped into them without boxers, his movements jerky and fast. I picked up my own pants, holding the phone to my ear with my shoulder.

Dad sighed. "We wanted to surprise you with a visit. We barely hear from you anymore, and your mother was worried. But all I really care about right now is where the hell—"

"*Hugh*." There was a commotion, something that sounded like a fight, and then Mom's voice came through. "Don't mind him. We know you're an adult now and you're out with friends. We missed you, dear. Where are you? We could come there to meet you and your friends."

"*No*." I shot Finn a desperate look, and he stepped into his motorcycle boots without a word. "I'll come to you. Just give me, like…?" I shot Finn a look and he held up his hand. "…five minutes, and I'll be there."

Mom sighed. "All right. I'll hold off your father. But hurry up, dear. I need a Carrie hug."

My heart wrenched with a bit of homesickness, despite the stress of the situation. That's what Mom called it when I hugged her as tight as I could. When I was a kid, every night she would pick me up and I would cling to her, all arms and legs and giggles, giving her the biggest good night hug I could.

When she let go and I stayed in place without her support, I would giggle harder—until I lost my grip and fell to the bed. Now I was too big to hang off her, but we still called our hugs *Carrie hugs*. "I'll hurry, I promise."

"Give me the phone, Margie."

"No."

"Give me the—" Another commotion. "And you'll be telling me who you were with," Dad called out. "Missy."

I could just picture him, pushing in to Mom to get another word in. Finn furiously typed something on his phone. Probably texting my dad in an attempt to cover both our asses before it was too late. Before Finn came under suspicion.

"Oh, leave her alone," Mom said. "See you soon."

"Bye," I said, hanging up. I looked at Finn. "What the heck are they doing here?"

"I don't have a fucking clue. I didn't know they were coming," Finn said, grabbing his keys and heading for the door with large, hurried steps. "Why didn't he tell me he was coming? This isn't good. This isn't good at all."

I followed him to the door, swallowing hard. Half my clothes were hung up in his closet and the other half were on his bed. I grabbed my empty bag. "I'll clean these up and then—"

Finn waved a hand and made an impatient sound. "Leave them. There's no time for that. We have to leave, and we have to leave yesterday."

I hesitated. "It'll be a little rough for a while, I get that, but why are you so upset?"

"Because I'm wondering why the fuck he didn't tell me he was coming, why the hell he hasn't texted me during the past two days, and why, even now, there's no text from him." His phone chimed, and he closed his eyes, his jaw ticking. "There it is."

He took his phone out of his pocket and opened the door for me. He scanned it and typed, while I tried to hold on to my patience. "What does it say?"

"He wants to know where you are." More typing. "I'm telling him you went out to eat with a new friend. Give me the name of someone you talk to in class. Someone new?"

I scrambled for the first name that came to mind. My lab partner I'd studied with the other day popped into my head. "Susan Williams."

"Good. He won't be able to locate her that quickly, so she's a good cover story. Your dad didn't tell me he's here in California, though." More typing, then he lifted his head. "Keep walking, Ginger. I can text and walk."

70

I clenched my fists. "I don't like this."

He didn't look up, just kept typing. "Don't like what?"

"You're acting different," I said, my voice cracking. "Again."

He'd barely looked at me at all since the phone call, and now he was acting cold. Distant. It freaked me out. Was he regretting the fact that he had me in his house when his boss came to visit? Kicking himself for being with me?

I didn't know, but I knew *something* was off.

He looked at me, his eyes as closed off as his voice. "Of course I am. I'm trying to cover our tracks. Your daddy's out there, thinking God knows what, doing God knows what, and I need to get you there without him knowing where the fuck you were. This is me in work mode, Ginger."

"He won't find out. You'll be fine."

"No, I won't be fine." He pressed his lips together, his nostrils flaring. "Because on *top* of that, the whole time he's here I have to stay the hell away from you when I don't even want to be away from you for a fucking minute. So, yeah, I'm a little bit distracted and cranky, to say the least."

He hauled me up against him and kissed me hard, not giving me a chance to reply. What would I have said anyway? What he said pretty much summed up my feelings, so instead, I clung to him, knowing we shouldn't be kissing like this in public, but unable to help myself.

I curled my hands into his shirt, twisting the fabric in my hands. I could feel the tears threatening to escape me, trying to run down my cheeks. But I wouldn't cry. It wasn't like this was goodbye or anything. It was a temporary setback—nothing and no one would make me walk away. Not even Dad.

He ended the kiss way too fast, resting his head on mine. "Let's get you back to your dad. Remember, if you see me watching you—don't even *look* at me. Act like you've never seen me before. Act like I'm no one and nothing. Don't save my name in your phone, and no incriminating texts."

"I can't even tell you I love you?" I asked, my throat swelling with the tears that were trying to escape.

"Not in those words. Text me…*the sun is finally shining*."

"The sun is finally shining?"

"Yeah. It's the first thing I thought of when I met you—that the sun was brighter and shiny and good."

My heart melted. How the heck was I supposed to walk away after that? "I don't want to go."

"I know." He kissed me one last time. "But you have to."

I stopped at the bike, but he tugged me past it. "Wait, where are you taking me?"

"You're taking a cab. I quietly called one while you were on the phone. We can't risk being seen together," he said matter-of-factly. When I opened my mouth to tell him no, he shook his head. "I know. It sucks, but it's how it has to be for now."

I blinked back tears. "Will you stay here?"

"No, I'm getting rid of your helmet and watching from the shadows, like I'm supposed to. And when your dad confronts me and asks where I was, I can tell him that I was watching you the whole time." He slapped my ass. "Now off you go, Ginger."

I walked to the cab, each step I took away from him becoming harder and harder. By the time I slipped into the seat, I was ready to turn around and bolt toward him. It was like something inside me thought this might be the last time I saw him. I didn't know what caused my racing heart and my fear, but it was tangible and undeniable.

And I somehow *knew* as the cab pulled away from the curb and Finn got rid of my helmet and climbed onto his bike...

Something was going to go terribly wrong.

CHAPTER ELEVEN

Finn

After I stashed Carrie's helmet inside my apartment in record speed, I hopped on my bike and followed the cab back to the dorms. I knew Carrie's parents were rich and a flight out didn't exactly break the bank or anything, but why had they come out all of a sudden? Had they just missed her, or was it something more?

Something like suspicion?

Maybe the senator had caught on to some weird vibe coming from across the fucking country and just instinctively known something was going on with his baby girl. But he couldn't. It's not like he was a psychic or some shit like that. He couldn't possibly know that I'd gotten a little bit *too* close in guarding his precious cargo.

…Could he?

Oh, fuck me. What if he'd sent over some extra security and I didn't even know about it? What if, right now even, he had a man watching *me*?

If he did, I was so screwed.

Carrie had thought she heard someone earlier. I had brushed it off, but maybe I'd been wrong. Maybe someone had been there, watching us and reporting back to her father from the shadows?

Son of a bitch…

I revved my engine, gripping the handlebars so tight it hurt, cursing myself ten times over for not considering this angle earlier. The cab pulled over and Carrie climbed out, her eyes seeking me out immediately. I parked my bike and tilted my head, telling her silently to look away and act like I didn't exist. Something told me she'd fail miserably. She wasn't a good liar, my Carrie, and it's one of the things I loved most about her—her honesty.

But it just might be our downfall.

She walked up to her parents, her steps quickening as she grew closer. After one last look over her shoulder at me, she ran into her mom's open arms. Her mom hugged her tight, burying her face in her hair and inhaling deeply. As if she missed Carrie's scent and needed to get as much of it as she could while she could.

Fuck, I got that. I got that all too well.

Next, her dad—the man I've never even seen crack a smile—grinned and hauled her into his arms, spinning her in a wide circle and saying something I couldn't make out. Carrie laughed in reply, the sound breaking through the night, and I closed my eyes.

Ah, that sound…

It had the power to save me from anything.

I watched from the shadows, my heart as heavy as a bowling ball in my chest. They looked so happy and normal right now. I had a hard time placing the man who was paranoid enough to send me to watch his daughter in secrecy with the man who stood here now, laughing and bussing Carrie's nose with a huge smile on his face.

And watching her in the arms of her parents just made our whole situation *real*. Would they ever welcome me into their family with open arms like that? All smiles and kisses and hugs? Doubtful. But I'd do my damned best to make it happen.

I'd make him accept me if it was the last thing I did, damn it.

The next morning, after an hour of watching Carrie bond with her parents and a mostly sleepless night, I woke up hung over and yet way too sober. I'd spent all night plotting and trying to come up with every possible scenario that could occur with her father's visit. I also tried to figure out why he was here.

And I failed.

I checked my text messages. One was from the senator. *I'm in town.*

It was a test. He knew I knew, but wanted to see what I said. *I saw you last night while I stood post. Welcome to California, sir.*

Thank you. Consider yourself off duty until I leave. I'll be in contact ASAP.

I clenched the phone. In other words? Stay away. *Looking forward to it, sir.*

I also had a text from Carrie. It was ridiculous how happy that made me. *The sun is finally shining today, Susan.*

I grinned. She'd saved me in her phone under a woman's name. How smart and devious. I liked it. *Indeed it is. You ready for chemistry class?*

I flopped back on my bed, resting my phone on my bare stomach as I waited for a reply. I didn't have to wait long. My phone vibrated, and I picked it up. *I prefer anatomy.*

Ha! Of course she did. That was our code for exploring each other's bodies, after all. I grinned. *Oh, me too. Believe me.*

As I waited for her to reply, I checked the time and realized she might not reply at all. She'd be walking into class right now, so she'd be silent for a while. Maybe I'd go to the beach. Ride a wave or two and try to figure out what was going on with my boss. Between the unusually quiet days leading up to this visit and the visit itself, I *knew* he knew something.

The question was *what*?

A knock sounded on the door, and I rolled out of bed wearing nothing but a pair of boxers. If someone wanted to knock on my door at this ungodly hour in the morning, then I reserved the right to open it half naked.

But when I opened the door, I wished I'd put some clothes on.

Senator Wallington, Carrie's father in the flesh, stood on my porch staring at me with what I could only describe as speculation in his eyes. Fucking sneaky bastard. I stepped in the doorway, not letting him inside. "Sir? I didn't realize you were texting me from my porch."

"I figured as much." He looked over my shoulder, so I closed the door even more. "Yet…here I am."

He craned his neck to try and see past me, but I didn't budge. Boss or not, he didn't get to drop in at my place unexpected like this. And Carrie's clothes were all over my room right now since I hadn't cleaned them up.

If he came in, he'd know. And I'd be done for.

"Is there something I can do for you, sir?"

"Yes." He crossed his arms over his flawless gray suit. Behind him, security stood in their black suits and shades, watching us both *Men in Black* style. Did I look that constipated when I stood behind the senator, not moving or talking? "You can let me inside, for starters."

I motioned down my body, my other hand gripping the door as tightly as I could. "It's a mess and I'm not dressed. I wasn't prepared for company."

"I don't care if it's a mess, and it's nothing I haven't seen before," he said simply, his voice perfectly calm. His eyes moved over my tattoos, seeming to fall upon each and every one. Then he snapped his attention to my face again. "Let me inside, Coram."

I knew he wouldn't walk away, and since he was my boss, I couldn't exactly refuse him entry. Fuck, I wanted to. Standing here talking to Carrie's dad while half naked with the scratches down my back that she'd made were perfectly visible was *not* my idea of a good start to my day.

I tugged on my hair and sighed. "You'll need to at least give me a second to pick up a little bit. Give me that much."

"You hiding something, Griffin Coram?"

I winced, hating the fact that I was being forced to lie again. I'd hoped my lying days were over when Carrie figured out who I was, yet here I was—lying through my teeth to her father—my boss. "No, sir. The only thing I'm hiding is a mess that I'd rather you not see."

He sighed impatiently. "Go on, then. Clean up and throw some clothes on. We'll go out to eat once you're clean enough."

I nodded and closed the door in his face, taking a second to brace myself for the upcoming confrontation. If he was taking me out to eat, then it couldn't be a bad thing that he was here, could it? Fuck if I knew.

I pushed off the door and made quick work of throwing on a pair of shorts and a T-shirt. Next, I tossed all of Carrie's clothes into a box, along with the pink hangers, and shoved it under my bed. After I made my bed, I stepped back and did a once-over of my place.

It looked Carrie-free again, unfortunately.

I smoothed my hands over my hair, took a calming breath, and opened the door. Senator Wallington still stood there, looking as poised as ever. I motioned him in. "If you'd like to come in now, you can."

The senator walked in, his gaze scanning the interior. His eyes seemed to touch upon anything and everything he could without digging through my drawers. I couldn't help but shift on my feet uneasily. Knowing my luck, I'd probably missed something. Maybe I'd left out a shirt or a hair tie.

He turned to me with his brows up. "This big enough for you? I can get you a bigger place if you prefer."

And just like that? The stress faded away. If he was talking about getting me a bigger apartment, I wasn't getting fired. It pretty much ruled out the possibility of there being another security guy out here with us. If he knew I was in love with his daughter, I would be at the business end of a fist right now.

Everything *had* to be okay. And my father would still get his retirement pension, and all was okay in the world. Minus the fact that I was a big fat fucking liar.

I forced a smile. "I'm fine here, sir. It's close to campus, and that makes my job easier."

"Good." He slid his phone into his pocket, his eyes on my bed. Could he tell that only a few hours earlier, his daughter had been with me in that bed he studied so closely? "Why do you have two surfboards in here?"

My breath slammed out of me. I eyed Carrie's blue surfboard and thanked God she didn't pick a girly one. "Why not? I like variety."

He gave me a hard look and sighed. "Let's go."

"After you, sir," I said quietly. I followed him outside, my palms sweating the whole time. I scanned the faces of the guards following the senator, then slid my shades onto my nose. "Cortez. Morris. Nice to see you again."

"You look different out of a suit, Coram," Morris said, his voice flat. "Like a surfer boy."

I *was* a surfer boy, but I kept my mouth shut on that matter.

"You look different *in* one while standing in California." I shrugged. "I need to blend in, so surfer boy I am."

"Makes sense," Cortez said.

"Yeah. How many of you are there out here?"

"Just us, to the best of my knowledge," Cortez said, his eyes on the senator, who walked in front of us. "But with the senator?" Cortez caught my gaze, not dropping it. "You never know."

Well, shit. That sounded an awful lot like a warning. "I'll remember that."

"You should," Cortez said, motioning me forward into the town car.

I nodded to both of them, then slid into the back of the car, settling into the far side of the seat to make room for all four of us. I kept replaying Cortez's words in my head, dissecting them and trying to make sense out of the whole thing.

My mind raced and my heart raced even faster. Was Cortez trying to warn me about something? Maybe he was trying to tell me that the senator had sent another man out here. If so, it would mean Carrie and I wouldn't even be able to be together. Could I handle that?

I'd been waiting to come clean for my father, but if I couldn't even see the woman I loved, would it be so cut and dry? Suddenly, I wasn't so sure about that.

When the senator sat beside me and closed the door, I blinked at him. "Where's the rest of your team, sir?"

"They'll watch Carrie today. After all, I have *you* with me."

"I don't even have my weapon, sir." I tapped my fingers on my knee. "It doesn't go with the clothes."

He waved a hand. "It's fine. I doubt we'll be attacked at breakfast."

"All right." I cocked a brow and buckled up, not sure how to take the senator's behavior. "She'll see them in those suits."

"I know." He shrugged and looked out the window, gripping the side of the door so tight his knuckles showed. His entire body screamed of impatience and anger and something a hell of a lot like *knowledge*. "She knows they're here now, so she won't question it."

Okay, he had a point, but she wouldn't like them being there. I fidgeted with my seatbelt, but forced myself to stop. It made me look guilty—which I was. Damn it, I hated this shit. Maybe I should come clean. Spit it out. Get it over with.

He wouldn't really cut off my father without a penny, would he? I didn't know, and I couldn't take that chance. If it were just me, I would open my mouth right now and tell him I loved his precious daughter. I'd accept the consequences of my actions. But with Dad months away from retirement, I couldn't take that chance.

I forced myself to nod. "That's true," I said, my voice stiff sounding even to my ears. "Do you have other guys besides me out here, sir?"

He looked at me, his eyes so like Carrie's it gave me the creeps. Even though they were the same shade, they were completely unreadable to me. He also had a way of staring me down that made me want to confess all my sins. Hard. Cold. *Calculated.*

He clenched his jaw. "Have you seen anyone else following Carrie lately?"

"Just thought I saw a few shadows moving." I shrugged. "Could've been my imagination."

"Keep an eye on it. As of now, you're the only one out here."

Thank fucking God. "I will, sir."

He tapped his fingers on the door. "If you need backup…"

"I don't. I'm fine." I adjusted my seatbelt again. "If that changes, I'll let you know."

"Are you juggling the Marines and my daughter with ease?"

Was it just me, or was that question rife with innuendo? "Yes, sir. I have to report for duty this weekend, but I'm sure she'll be fine without me watching her. She's proved to have a remarkably good head on her shoulders. You must be very proud of her."

The senator smoothed his jacket, a look of pride taking over his face. Not a smile, but the closest thing I've ever seen from him that wasn't directed toward his family. "Indeed, I am."

"As well you should be, sir."

He looked out the window. "Your father says hello."

I swallowed hard. Part of me had hoped he would have come here, too. I missed him. "I look forward to seeing him once I return home for the holidays."

"He was going to come along, but something got in the way." The senator turned away, his jaw hard but his eyes somehow softer. "Something unavoidable."

"Oh?" I loosened my seatbelt, my heart quickening at the odd reply. I hadn't heard from my father a whole lot lately, and it hadn't even registered on my radar with all the other shit I had going on, but now it was glaringly clear. "And what would that be? Is everything okay with him, sir?"

He looked back my way, and the momentary flash of emotion had dissipated. The relentless politician I was accustomed to had returned. "I think that's something you need to talk to him about."

That didn't sound fucking good at all. What unavoidable thing could my father have had come up? "I'll call him after breakfast, sir."

"Good." Senator Wallington looked out the window again, giving me a reprieve from the nonstop scrutiny. I'd never seen the man so damned restless before. "I have to say, I had my suspicions in coming out here. Suspicions that led me to come out here directly."

And just like that, my heart stopped beating, then painfully accelerated. "Sir?"

"I knew Carrie was hiding something. I came here because I knew she wasn't being completely honest with me, and now I know what she's hiding."

My chest squeezed tight. "What would that be, sir?"

"Don't you know already?" He leaned closer, eyeing me like a predator with its prey. "I think you do. I think you know exactly what I want to know, and you're going to tell me every detail without leaving a single thing out."

"I don't know what you want to hear from me, sir," I forced myself to say. My voice sounded pretty damn calm. I leaned back against the seat, even though I wanted to bolt and warn Carrie. My heart pounded in my ears, echoing like a drum solo in an empty room. "I've been doing my job. Watching your daughter. Keeping her out of trouble."

He leaned forward and gripped my shoulder far too hard to be comforting. "Well, tell me everything you know."

This was it. This was the fucking beginning of the end. Even knowing this, I forced myself to calmly ask, "About *what*, sir?"

He narrowed his eyes at me, for once not looking cold. No, he looked fucking pissed off. "Why don't *you* tell me?"

CHAPTER TWELVE

Carrie

Mom tilted her head, fingering the sleeve of the soft teal sweater in front of her. "I don't know, honey. Which one do you think you'll get the most use out of?"

"I like this one," I said, my mind not really on the sweater. It was on Finn and the chemistry homework I'd never finished, and the lab I had to do tomorrow morning. "It's a lighter shade."

Mom nodded. "And feel how soft it is."

I sighed, reaching out and touching the soft sweater, trying my best to look as into the whole shopping experience as she was. I'd never been able to last as long as she could, and today was no exception. We'd been shopping for three hours, and I was *done*. D-O-N-E, *done*. I didn't care which one she bought thirty minutes ago, and I didn't care now either.

It was a shirt. A shirt Finn would undoubtedly rip off me at some point.

"It'll go better with your hair." She held the sweater up to me, and I held my arms out as she studied my complexion. "Yes, this'll do. Now, for some pants..."

I followed her, barely biting back a groan. Truth be told, I wasn't much of a shopper, but she was, and it made her happy. I smiled and acted as if I cared what color socks I wore with my sweaters because it made *her* smile. As she combed through a rack of black jeans, I peeked over my shoulder for the ten-millionth time.

Finn still wasn't out there. Just a pair of suits.

Where was he? Was I just not seeing him? For a while after our big fight, he'd done a good job at staying hidden from me. Maybe he was incognito or something.

"Oh, look at the pockets on these." Mom pulled out a pair of black jeans with zippers on a bunch of pockets from the back of the rack. "They look like something a biker chick would wear, don't you think?"

They did. I could easily picture myself sitting on Finn's bike, wearing those pants and wrapping my arms around his waist. I bet he'd like them, too. For the first time this whole shopping trip, my heart picked up speed. "Yeah, and I like them. Are they my size?"

She looked at me with a raised brow. "Of course they are. I wouldn't have pulled them out if they weren't."

"I'll take them." I smiled at her, my eyes still on the pants. "Thanks, Mom."

"You're welcome, dear." She pursed her lips and looked at me, her eyes narrowed. I stiffened. Last time she looked at me like that, I'd been forced to get a haircut because it was fresh and fun. I'd hated it. "Shall we get you some biker boots to go with it?"

I tensed. She sounded *suspicious*. As if she knew I was riding a bike now. She couldn't possibly know that. I forced myself to relax and smile. "Um, sure. Why not? They're fashionable now. Maybe with some laces that go all the way up?"

She tapped a finger on her lip. "Your tastes have changed."

"I've grown up." I looked over my shoulder, searching the crowd outside for Finn. Still no sign of him. I turned back to Mom. "Is that so bad?"

She smiled and headed for the register. "Of course not. As a matter of fact, I think I like the changes. You look happier."

That's because I was. I had Finn. "I am, Mom. Really, *really* happy."

"Good. And I'm glad you're free of all the stresses from our life out here." Mom stood in line, tapping her foot as she waited. "Last week, we hosted three senators and a governor for dinner. Everything was rolling along smoothly, but then, wouldn't you know it? Christy got the flu and couldn't make the dinner. We had to scramble for a replacement chef at the last second, and Dad was on a rampage."

I flinched. I was all too familiar with the stresses that came with being a Wallington. "Who did you find?"

"The Stapletons loaned us theirs. He was delightful." Mom looked over her shoulder, her eyes lighting up. "Hey, you remember them, right? They have a son who's a couple of years older than you. His name's Riley."

I scanned my memory. I vaguely remembered a guy a few years older than me at Dad's last gala, but to be honest, most of those events passed in a blur. "Blond hair, green eyes, and tall?"

"Mmhm." She smiled even bigger. "You remember him."

"Yeah, sure." I shrugged. "He seemed nice enough."

"Well, he wants to go sailing with you over the summer break." Mom stepped forward in the line a little bit more. "They visited the night of the disaster, and we got to talking about you. You'll never believe it, but he goes to school upstate, near San Francisco."

I tensed. Why hadn't I realized where this was going? "Mom…"

"Oh relax, dear." She patted my arm. "It's a sailing expedition, not a betrothal."

I choked on a laugh. "I know, but I'm not looking for a boyfriend right now." *Because I already have one.* "Besides, why would he be thinking about taking me out? He doesn't even really *know* me."

"Your father and his are in the same political party, as you know, so it's an advantageous move for both families." She sighed and hugged the clothes tighter to her chest. "You do know at one point, you'll have to come home and play the game. Be the daughter your father needs you to be. Right?"

I stiffened and swallowed hard. In other words, I was expected to come home and marry a Stapleton like a good little girl. Yeah. That wasn't going to happen. I didn't need a *Stapleton*. I had a *Coram*. This was exactly what Finn had been worried about. And I'd laughed it off, as if it didn't matter and would never come into play.

I'd been wrong. It did matter. Finn was smart to plan ahead.

"Mom, I'm not marrying someone to further Dad's career," I said, my voice low. "I love you, and I love him, but *no*."

"You're not going to marry a man for your father. That's not what I meant." She shrugged. "But you'll marry someone who will be a benefit to the family, I'm sure. Someone who is worthy of standing beside a Wallington. You should take more pride in who you are."

"I have plenty of pride." I crossed my arms. "But you have too much. We're no different than anyone else."

"I didn't say we were. You're putting words in my mouth." Mom sighed. "It's hard to see the big picture when you're so young." She reached out and squeezed my arm, her eyes kind, even though her words made me want to scream. "You have time. There's no rush for you to accept this all right here."

I clenched my teeth. I wouldn't be accepting it ever. "*Mom.*"

"It's about more than what we want out of life. There's your father's career, the presidential campaign, the opportunities…you're just too young to see that." Mom dropped her arm. "Looks like it's my turn to pay."

Mom stepped forward and chatted up the store employee, acting for all the world as if she hadn't just dropped a bombshell on me and walked away. I fidgeted and looked over my shoulder. Dad was out there talking to the suits, but still no Finn.

Not able to stand it another second, I pulled out my phone and texted him. *Everything okay, Susan?*

My phone buzzed and my heart sped up. *Yeah, I'm fine. What are you up to?*

I peeked at Mom, making sure she wasn't watching me. Luckily, she was too busy chatting. *Shopping with my mom.*

Oh boy. Sounds…fun? Okay. I can't lie. Not really. You know I'm not much of a shopper.

I held back a smile. *Yeah, I know.*

Are you going to buy something pretty?

I grinned. *Like…?*

I don't know. A skirt for church? Maybe we could share it.

I snorted, then glanced up cautiously. Mom was almost finished. *Uh-oh. We're done paying. I have to go.*

Okay. Hey, the sun is finally shining.

I looked out the window and smiled. *It really is.*

I shoved my phone back in my pocket just in time for Mom to stop yakking to the cashier. She looked at me, taking in my flushed cheeks more than likely. She arched a dainty brow. "What were you doing, dear?" she asked.

I scrambled for something to say and blurted out the first thing that came to mind. "Looking at used cars."

"Cars?" Mom blinked at me. "Do you want one?"

I nodded frantically, wiping my sweaty palms on my thighs. "Yeah, someday. Something inexpensive to get around in, you know? I spend a lot in cab fare."

"Okay." She shrugged. "Tell your father. He'll buy you one."

"I will." *Not.* If I told him, he'd buy me some expensive, top-of-the-line car. I wanted something old and rusty. Nothing fancy. I cleared my throat, ready to change the subject. "By the way, how's your friend Mary? The one who went for surgery on Monday when we talked?"

"Oh, I think she's better."

I nodded, letting her walk in front of me and following her closely. "How do you know? Did you go see her again?"

"No. She's back on our *Words With Friends* game as of an hour ago." Mom looked back at me and shrugged. "She can't play if she's not feeling better, so she must be fine."

I choked on a laugh. "Uh…yeah. I guess so."

I followed her out the door, my attention focused on Dad. I looked for any signs of anger or frustration or knowledge, but he just smiled at me and hugged Mom. When he hugged me, kissing the top of my head like he always did, I wanted to shake him and ask him where Finn was. I couldn't.

I had to play the game.

"Where have you been?" I asked him.

I looked up at him like I used to do when I was a little girl, with my chin resting on his chest. It took me back to a time when I'd thought he could do no wrong. I'd thought he was perfect back then. Invincible. How naïve I'd been. He was a good man. He really was. But he had flaws like the rest of us.

"You weren't done until three and I knew your mother wanted to go shopping with you like old times." He eyed the bags in my hands and Mom's. "Looks like you were both successful."

"Of course we were," Mom said, fluffing her light red hair. "But where'd you run off to all day, Hugh?"

"Oh, you know, taking care of some business." Dad averted his eyes and let go of me, pressing his lips together. His dark brown hair was immaculately in place, and he was clean-shaven. If he smiled, he'd flash those famous dimples that made all the women in America swoon. He could probably win the campaign with those two assets alone. "I'm starving. You two ready to eat something?"

I nodded. "Sure."

"Absolutely," Mom said.

He grinned, his dimples popping out. "All right. Off we go, the fearsome threesome."

I didn't follow him as he walked, and it took him all of two seconds to notice. When he turned to me with a curious expression, I gave him a level look. A few months ago, I wouldn't have had the courage to stand up to him like this, but I'd changed. Finn had shown me how life was supposed to be, and it wasn't *this*. "Lose the suits. I'm not ruining my cover because you're scared we'll be attacked at the restaurant."

If Finn still followed us, Dad wouldn't even hesitate to send the men packing. He would shrug and tell them to go eat. "You know I can't do that."

"Sure you can. Normal people do it all the time."

"We're not normal," he stressed, looking pointedly at Mom. "A little help here, Margie?"

"But—"

"*I* am normal when I'm here." I caught his gaze, biting down on my lip so hard it hurt. He wasn't sending them away. This wasn't good. Wasn't good at all. "Back home I follow all your rules, even though it kills me to be so freaking sheltered. Out here, you need to follow mine. You promised I could be normal here."

His tough façade cracked. "Carrie…"

"Please?" I curled my hands into fists, not dropping my gaze. "Daddy?"

Yep. I pulled out the big guns. Worked every time.

"Hugh…" Mom grabbed his elbow, holding on tight. "They can take our bags home, dear. It'll be fine. Plus, it'll be nice with just the three of us."

Dad released a breath and motioned them over. "You can take our bags and head back to the hotel. We'll be there after dinner."

The security man nodded, took our bags, and motioned for his buddy to follow him. He wore the same black suit they always wore, and I tried to picture Finn standing beside them perfectly immobile and serious.

The image of the Finn I knew didn't mesh well with the security guard Finn, but I knew that's what he was. What he did. "Thanks, Dad."

"You're welcome," he said, his voice gruff.

Mom grinned, looking back and forth between us. "So, where are we going?" Mom asked, linking her arm with Dad's.

I forced myself to pay attention. "There's a great burger place called Islands. We could—"

"Burgers?" Mom snorted. "I don't think so, Carrie."

Dad looked down at her. "I hear there's a great five-star sushi place in town. Let's go there. Sound good, Carrie?"

No. I hated sushi, and he knew it. Or at least…he should. Then again, maybe I'd never bothered to mention it to him. But there would be something besides sushi at the restaurant, so I could work with it. "Sure. That sounds great."

"What time are your classes tomorrow?" Dad asked.

I had to think about it for a second. "Nine to four."

"Any plans afterward?" Mom asked, her eyes on mine.

"Nope."

Dad stiffened. "Do we have to do this right here, Margie?"

I looked at both of them, unable to follow whatever the heck was going on right now. I slid into the town car and waited for them both to be seated before answering. "I'd assumed I would be hanging out with you two, since you're only here until Saturday night."

"No hot date?" Mom asked, a smile on her face.

She wasn't making any sense. One second she's asking me to come home and marry a Stapleton, and the next she's asking me if I have a hot date planned. I blinked at her. "Uh…no? Why?"

"Well…" Mom smiled even wider, but Dad grew even tenser, if possible. "Your father thinks you're dating someone and hiding it. And I *hope* you are. Well, the dating part. Not the hiding, because I want to hear all about him. We all need to have some fun in college before settling down."

Ah. So that's why she was acting all happy to hear about the possibility of me dating someone. She viewed it as a fling or sowing wild oats or something equally untrue. I gripped my knees so tight it hurt, focusing on Dad instead of her. "Why would you think I'm seeing someone?"

"I have my reasons." He looked over at me, pinning me against the door without even touching me. "Are you?"

My heart beat so loudly in my ears I couldn't hear anything but my own panicked thoughts. "N-No…?"

Oh my God, did he know? *Could* he know? Had Finn told him?

He tilted his head. "Is that a question or an answer?"

"An answer," I said, straightening my spine. If I was going to save Finn's job and keep his father employed through his last few months, then I needed to do better at lying. I tried to ignore my racing pulse. "Of course it's an answer. What kind of question is that, anyway?"

"The question of a concerned father."

"Well, my *concerned father* needs to realize I'm not a little girl anymore, and he needs to relax." When he opened his mouth to argue, I shot him a look that probably could have set coals on fire. "And this goes for you, too, Mom. I'll date who I want, when I want, and I won't answer to either one of you for it."

Mom gasped, covering her mouth. "Carrie, don't yell at us."

I closed my eyes for a second. I hadn't even raised my voice in the slightest. "I'm not yelling. I'm simply letting you two know that *if* and *when* I'm dating a man, I'll bring him to meet you when I'm good and ready. Not a second before. You flying out here to check on me and try to catch me in a lie isn't going to hurry me up any. You don't like that? Then stop trying to dig into something that isn't your business. Last time I checked, I was a legal adult. I expect to be treated as such."

Mom's eyes went wider, and Dad turned red...then even redder. I never stood up to them like this, so I got the shock they were experiencing—but dude, it felt good. Really, *really* good. "You listen to me, young lady, you'll—"

Mom squeezed his arm, but didn't look away from me. "Dear? I think this discussion is better ended right here and now. I know that look in her eye all too well. Let it go."

"But I—" He broke off and pointed at me. "And she—"

Mom patted his arm. "I know, Hugh. It's called growing up. Kids do that."

"They don't talk to their parents like that," he huffed. "If I'd done that to my father, I wouldn't have been able to sit straight for a week."

The car stopped in front of the restaurant, but none of us moved. "I love you both very much," I said softly, "but *some* things have to be done in my time, on my terms. That's all I'm asking."

Dad pressed his lips together, looking as if he wanted nothing more than to shout, but he nodded. "Fine. If you choose the wrong man, I will do everything in my power to send him packing."

I had no doubt that Finn was probably the "wrong guy" in Dad's eyes, but nothing would send Finn running. I was confident in his love for me, and in our love for each other. "You can try."

He narrowed his eyes on me. "Are you at least going to tell me who he is?"

"There is no 'he' at all," I stated, opening the door. "Now let's go eat."

I heard my mother whisper something to my father, and he answered back in hushed tones. When they climbed out of the car, he looked even more pissed off, but he was quiet. I couldn't shake the sinking suspicion that Dad knew more than he was letting on—that he was playing us both against one another until one of us broke and gave away our secrets. It wouldn't be me.

I was determined to keep my silence, my freedom, and my Finn…

No matter what I had to do.

CHAPTER THIRTEEN

Finn

Friday night I tossed all my shit into the green field bag on my bed, my mind at least a million miles from this damn drill weekend. It had been two days since I last saw Carrie, and I was like a man detoxing from heroin. I had the shakes and I needed her *now*. If I could hold her for one minute, and inhale her sweet scent, it would be enough to get me through the weekend. Just a small fix.

I hugged her sweater she'd left here, holding it to my nose to inhale deeply. It wasn't enough. I needed more. I needed *her*. But I couldn't have her until her parents left. It was fucking ridiculous that I was so impatient considering the fact that it would only be a few days apart. It shouldn't be so damn hard to be without her.

But it really fucking was.

Even worse? Her father suspected I was hiding something.

I *was*, but I couldn't say it yet. Not until my father retired. And the really shitty part about this plan? My silence would only make him hate me in the end.

I couldn't betray my own father. Not even for my own chance at happiness.

Knowing I'd possibly lost the one chance I had to come clean with the man didn't exactly sit well, but it was my *dad*. What was I supposed to do? Throw him under the tires to save myself? Over my dead body.

Still, it sucked ass.

My phone rang, and I crossed the room to pick it up off my bed. Once I saw the number, I relaxed a bit. I'd called my father the other day, after the cryptic lunch with Senator Wallington, but he hadn't called me back. Dad *always* called me back right away. "Hey, Dad. It's about time you returned my call."

"Hello, son. I heard that you—" he cleared his throat and continued, "that you were getting company out there."

"Yeah. I kind of expected you to come." I reclined on my bed, Carrie's sweater still in my hands. I absentmindedly ran my fingers over the bandage covering my chest. I'd gotten new ink today. "And don't avoid the question. Why didn't you call me back?"

I played with her sweater as I waited for Dad to answer. He sounded sluggish tonight. He made a weird moaning sound. "I wasn't invited to come along, and I was busy."

I cocked a brow. "Doing what? Guarding the dog? The rest of them are here."

Dad laughed. "You know how much they love this stupid thing. He asked me to stay behind and take care of her."

That was a lie. Dad *never* lied to me.

"You were invited. The senator told me," I replied, sitting up straight. "He said you were going to come out, but something came up. Then I call, and it takes you two days to get back to me? Tell me the truth—what's up, Dad?"

"Oh. Okay, then." Dad sighed, sounding old and tired even through the phone. "I'm sick. I have a pretty nasty flu. It's knocked me down pretty hard."

Well, that explained the weak tone of his voice, at least, and the non-visit. I rolled to my feet and went back to packing, balancing the phone on my shoulder and tossing Carrie's sweater on my pillow. "Oh, that sucks. Are you on the upswing yet?"

He laughed lightly. "I'm trying."

"Do you want me to let you go to bed? You know rest is the best thing for a flu, right?" I ran a hand over my short hair. I'd gotten it cut earlier this morning. "That and the chicken noodle soup Mom used to make, of course."

"I am. And I do." He coughed lightly, then laughed. "It's not as bad as it sounds. I feel fine most of the time. It just gets worse at night."

He didn't sound fucking fine to me. My heart picked up speed. The sound of his weak voice brought back bad memories of Mom lying in bed, slowly wasting away till nothing was there but death. "Are you s-sure? I could come home and check on you—"

"*No*," he said, his voice perfectly strong that time. "I'm fine. You focus on your job and stop worrying about me and my stupid virus."

Which reminded me about the call I'd gotten—and the possible deployment. I couldn't tell him that shit when he was sick. It could be nothing. And if it *was* something, then I'd tell him about it after this weekend. I didn't want him losing sleep when he needed the rest. "If you're sure…"

"I am." He cleared his throat again, sounding like he choked back a cough at the same time. "I'm going to go now. I love you."

I swallowed hard. He sounded like shit. "I love you, Dad."

I hung up the phone and started to set it down, but my phone vibrated in my hand. A text from Carrie. *You home?*

I sighed and tried to brush off the phone call with my father. He was sick, but he'd get better and be back to his happy self soon enough. *Yeah. Packing for cheerleading camp. You?*

I grinned as soon as I hit send. She'd get a kick about where I said I'd be going, and I couldn't wait to see what her reply was. But it didn't come.

A few minutes passed, making me grow twitchy and forget all about my dad's cold. Lately, the texts had been shorter and fewer, making me wonder if she was already pulling away from me. Then I remembered she was with her parents, and I kicked myself in the nuts for being such a neurotic fucking mess all the time.

My phone buzzed and I looked down at it with a hunger that was laughable. Who the hell got so excited to get a fucking text? *I'm home.*

I pictured her lying in her dorm bed, all alone in a pair of skimpy shorts and a tank top. Was her hair down or in a ponytail? My heart squeezed tight. I shouldn't miss her this much, damn it. It had only been a few days of no contact. We'd gone longer before, but that had been before we became a couple.

I guess that made a difference in my tolerance. I shook my head and focused on my phone. *Going to bed now?*

Barely a second passed. *Maybe...*

It's either a yes or a no. What's the hesitance?

Hold on.

The key sounded in the door, and I lurched to my feet. The only other person with a key was Carrie. And if Carrie was here...I didn't know whether to kiss her or yell at her for being so damn reckless. With her parents in town, the last place she should be is with me.

Her father had said no one was watching us, but that didn't mean he wasn't lying. The man was more slippery than an eel in salt water. I didn't trust him one bit. She walked in, closing the door behind her quickly, her eyes locking with mine. All that mattered was she was here.

A fist of emotion knocked the breath right out of me, making it hard to breathe. I took a stumbling step toward her, then another. Yeah. I wasn't going to yell at her. I was going to kiss her and hold her and thank God she came to see me because I'd missed her way too much. My fingers itched with the need to touch her, to have her.

All I could manage to say, amidst all the feelings she brought to life with her reappearance, was one word. "*Carrie.*"

"Before you say anything, I know I'm not supposed to be here." She leaned against the door and breathed heavily, her eyes on mine. Her gaze dipped lower, lingering on the bandage on my chest, but then she tore her eyes away. "But I have a car now. Dad bought it for me. I told Mom I wanted one and the next day it was there. It's ridiculous how easy it was, but it got me here, and that's all that matters."

I blinked at her. She had a car now? I hadn't even known she *wanted* one.

She continued on, obviously not needing a reply from me. "I parked at the store down the street. Then I went inside, left through the back, and walked here. I won't stay long, so no one will guess where I am. Don't yell at me."

I opened and closed my fists. "Why would I yell at you when I could kiss you instead?"

"Then do it already," she said, her eyes flashing at me.

I let out a broken sound I didn't even recognize and closed the distance between us. I didn't stop until I had her pinned against the door, my body glued to hers. I ran my hands all over her, starting at her shoulder, then dipping down her side and brushing against her breast.

Her breath hitched in her throat, and I yanked her against my body, knowing I should be sending her away but unable to.

Because I was fucking lost.

"You're really here," I breathed. "It's not another dream."

"I'm really here." She tilted her face up, her nails digging into my chest. "Are you going to kiss me or not?"

I groaned and closed my mouth over hers, slipping my tongue inside her lips as if I were a starving man and she was my last supper. And if she was? Well, at least I'd die a happy man. She let out a whimper and clung to me harder, her tiny nails piercing my skin. I couldn't give a damn.

She could draw blood from me as often as she wanted, as long as she was *here*.

Our kiss seemed to break something inside of me. I growled as I lifted her against the door, my hands on her waist. As I undid the button, she trembled and grabbed her shirt, breaking off the kiss long enough to rip it over her head before fusing her mouth to mine once more.

I tugged her shorts over hips, letting them hit the floor, then slid my hand between her legs, expecting to feel the smooth satin of her underwear. Instead, I touched bare skin, and I shuddered with the need that punched through me. It would drive me fucking insane from now on—wondering whether she had anything on under her fucking pants.

I let go of her and crossed the room in record speed, grabbing a condom out of my drawer and tearing it open impatiently. After I had the protection aspect of what we were about to do under control, I stepped between her legs and lifted her higher against the door. I wanted to take it slow and be all seductive and romantic and shit, but she was driving me insane with the little noises she was making and the way her hips rose toward me, begging for more. And I was a desperate man.

I broke off the kiss, my breathing harsh and my cock positioned at her pussy. "This isn't going to be sweet or soft. Are you okay with that?"

"Yes." She buried her hands in what was left of my hair and wrapped her legs around my waist. "Just hurry *up*, damn it."

I groaned and kissed her again, plunging inside of her in one smooth thrust. When I was buried inside her all the way, I tightened my grip on her and pressed her against the door even harder to make sure she had good support. Then…I fucking lost all control. I pulled out of her and thrust back inside—hard and fast and rough. And I didn't stop.

She clung to me, crying out my name. For a second I thought I hurt her, and started to pull back, but she dug her heels into my ass and held me in place, her hips moving restlessly against me. "Don't...stop."

I growled and plunged inside of her again, even harder. I wanted to tell her how much she meant to me, and how much I needed her in my life, but all I could do was move inside of her, making her moan and scream out my name and draw my blood.

Her nails raked down my chest to my abs, leaving a stinging sensation behind them, and I drove deeper inside of her. Her hands faltered over my bandage, but she closed her eyes and lost herself in the rhythm. When she started trembling, her thighs quivering around me, I positioned myself so that I brushed against her clit with each thrust and bit down on her neck. Within seconds, her pussy clenched around me and she tensed, her whole body going tight and hard.

I pounded into her once, twice, and one more time, my entire body shutting down from the force of the orgasm rocking through me. I collapsed against her, still supporting her weight with one arm, and dropped my head against the door by her shoulder. She breathed as unevenly as I did, and she held me close, her arms tight around me.

I didn't want to ever move. I wanted to stay like this, buried inside of her against my fucking apartment door. Because once I moved, I knew she would have to leave, and I'd be alone again, with nothing but my thoughts to keep me company.

She lifted her head from my shoulder, looking up at me with her bright blue eyes. "I think we needed that. These past few days have been rough."

"I know. I never thought I'd be one of those guys who needed his girl with him to be happy, but..." I shrugged and smiled at her. "I am now, and I don't mind. What did you do to me, Ginger?"

"I don't know, but you did it to me, too." She blew her hair out of her face and eyed me. "What's up with the bandage? You okay?"

I sighed and lifted her off the door, setting her down on her feet gently. She clung to me for a second, then seemed to gain her footing. Bending down, I picked up her shorts and handed them to her. "Yeah. I'm fine. Where's your dad right now?"

She gave me a lopsided grin. "Probably still recovering from me yelling at him. I kind of told him to mind his own business from now on." She stepped into the shorts and buttoned them, then took her shirt out of my hand and smiled her thanks. "Went all independent woman on him and everything."

"Man, I would've paid to see that." I snorted, picturing the look on her dad's face while Carrie told him off. "I bet he didn't know what to say."

"Oh, he definitely didn't." She pulled the shirt over her head and leaned against the door, right where I'd fucked her. I would never be able to look at a door again without getting a hard-on. "It was pretty funny. I should have taken a picture of his face for you."

I pulled on my shorts and sat down on the edge of my bed, not bothering with a shirt, and held my arms out for her. "Come here, Ginger. I can't stand not having you in my arms for another second."

She crossed the room and sat in my lap, curling up against my chest in a little ball. She rested her hand over my chest, right above my new tat. "Now *answer* me. What's with the bandage?"

"I got new ink."

She perked up at that. "Cool. Show me?"

I grinned and hugged her closer. "I will in a minute. Right now I just want to hold you before I send you back to your dad."

"Do you think he knows about us?"

I sighed, carefully choosing my words. "I think he knows you're seeing someone, but he doesn't know who."

She placed her hand over my heart. "Did he ask you if I'm seeing anyone?"

I nodded and rested my cheek on top of her head. She didn't smell like my shampoo. For some reason, that made me sad. "He did. I told him I'd seen you with a few guys, but they all seemed to be just friends. I said you were focusing on your studies for the most part."

"A *few* guys?" She slapped my arm hard. "You made me sound like a slut?"

I laughed. "I said they were friends."

"But you made—"

"Oh, shut it already." I tossed her onto the bed and climbed on top of her, laughing and kissing her into silence. When she was clinging to me and squirming beneath me, I pulled back and looked down at her. Everything from her flushed cheeks to her swollen lips screamed for me to keep her here, under me, but I knew I couldn't. So I did the first thing that came to mind.

I tickled her.

For a second, I wondered if she wasn't ticklish. She just stared up at me with narrowed eyes, but then her eyes went wide, a whoosh of air left her lungs, and she broke into laughter, squirming and begging me to stop. I joined her, laughing my ass off and tickling harder.

Only once tears were streaming down her face and she was begging for mercy did I stop, and she still laughed, clinging to me. We both struggled to catch our breath, and I rolled onto the side, holding her close. "You're extremely ticklish, Ginger."

She took a shaky breath, finally seeming to have herself under control. "I had no idea. I've never been tickled."

"Seriously?" I asked her incredulously. Well, I guess I shouldn't be too surprised. The senator didn't exactly seem the tickling type, but I'd thought her mother might have been… I guess not. My own mother had been. "I'm going to tickle you all the time now."

"God, no." She laughed lightly but pressed her lips together, her eyes on my bag. "Are you going to show me your tattoo before I have to go?"

I hesitated. It was the most telling piece I'd gotten since I got Mom's birthdate on my shoulder. "Yeah. Soon."

She ran her fingers over my head lightly. "You cut your hair, huh?"

I kissed her gently. "Yep. I have to report for duty in the morning."

"I know," she said, her eyes still on the bag. She sighed and looked away, her gaze on my pillow. "Are you bringing my shirt with you?"

I arched my neck, spotting the purple sweater I'd been hugging earlier. My cheeks heated, and I debated whether to admit why it was there. Would she think it was pathetic or sweet? If I told another guy, he'd call me names *I* didn't even say out loud.

But this was Carrie.

"Well, you see…" I cleared my throat. Something told me I was turning in my man-card by admitting this, but fuck it. I didn't need it. "I missed you. So I may or may not have been sniffing your sweater right before you came."

Tears filled her eyes and she wrapped her arms around my neck. "That's way too cute."

"Are you sure?" I kissed her, keeping it light and sweet. "It might just be creepy."

"I'm positive as a proton that it's cute and not even the slightest bit creepy."

I chuckled. "I missed hearing that phrase…." I trailed off and kissed her neck, desperately breathing in her scent so I could carry it with me all weekend. "Did you want to see my ink now?"

"Uh, *yeah*," she said, craning her neck and trying to peek. "I've only been begging for the past five minutes. What is it?"

I peeled it back enough for her to see. "It's our tattoo."

I watched her as she read it, her mouth silently moving along as she read the words. It was in a script-type scrawl: *the sun is finally shining*. It was over my heart, which was fitting since she owned it.

"It's perfect." She looked up at me, tears in her eyes. "I want one, too. When you get back, you'll take me. Got it?"

"You want ink?"

"I do. I want that one." She ran her fingers over it gently, making sure not to hurt me. It was still raised and red and covered in the antibacterial goo, but I didn't tell her not to touch it. I didn't give a damn. "That same exact one."

"Then you'll have it." I kissed her gently. After grabbing her hand, I helped her to her feet and hugged her tight, my heart hammering away at the idea of her walking away from me. "But now you have to go. Don't miss me too much while I'm gone."

"I'm not making any promises." She buried her face in my chest. "Hey, where are the rest of my clothes?"

"Under the bed. You can hang them back up once your parents are gone."

"I will." She hugged me tighter, obviously as reluctant as me to let go. "Do I *have* to go?"

I wanted to say no. I wanted to tell her she could stay, her father be damned. But I knew it wasn't the right thing to do, even if it felt like it right now. "You do."

"But the sun is finally shining," she said, her voice muffled because she had her face pressed against my bare chest.

My heart fisted painfully, making it hard to breathe. "It really fucking is." My fingers flexed on her, but I forced myself to let go. "I'll follow you from a distance, okay?"

"Okay." She bit her lip. "But it's only a two-minute walk to my car. I'll be fine."

"The day I let you walk around at night by yourself is the day I'll be dead in a coffin." Which reminded me… "Are you going to the soup kitchen with Marie?"

She nodded. "Yeah, I think so. I have tons of McDonald's gift cards sitting in my room."

"That's fine, but leave before dark—no matter what." I shooed her out the door. "Now get that perfect ass walking out that door so I can follow you."

She gave me one last longing look, then opened the door and left without another word. I silently slid out of my apartment about ten seconds later and followed her. She didn't acknowledge my existence, but she knew I was there.

When she got in her car—which turned out to be a used 2003 Mercedes SL500—and drove off, she craned her neck to watch me until I worried she'd crash into a telephone pole. I had to tackle the desire to chase after her car and drag her back to my apartment where she fucking belonged.

I leaned against the wall in the alleyway and closed my eyes. I couldn't believe how much a man could change in the blink of an eye. Before her, I didn't want a relationship or love. I wanted to focus on work and life before settling down, *if* I ever did. Now, all I could think about was love and marriage and babies and all the shit that came when you signed your heart away to another person. And yet, amidst all of the dreams, hopes, and desires, I knew that this time tomorrow…

I would find out whether our love would withstand what the world was going to throw our way.

Carrie

I crept up the stairs to my dorm, my heart racing as I hid in the shadows. I was fairly certain Dad's guards hadn't caught on to my ruse, but with them, you never knew. They were all sneaky bastards that made a living off following you around. And they were *good* at it, too. After all, Dad only hired the best.

I slipped into my dorm room, closing the door behind me quietly. As I leaned against it, I pulled out my phone and shot off a quick text to Finn to let him know I got home all right. He replied immediately, wishing me a good night, and I closed my eyes, holding my phone to my chest.

Going to see him had been a risky move.

But he was leaving tomorrow morning, and I'd missed him, and it had to happen. I was terrified that once he showed up tomorrow, he wouldn't be coming back. Scared that something or someone wouldn't let him. He couldn't leave me.

I pushed off the door and crossed the room quietly. I peeked in the direction of Marie's bed, but it was empty. Guess I didn't have to be so quiet. I flopped back on the bed and looked up at the dark ceiling. I should probably shower or something, but I didn't want to move.

I kept replaying the short visit with Finn over and over in my head, like a baby's lullaby. He'd actually gotten a tattoo for us. That was huge for him. We didn't talk much about his tattoos, but I knew each one had a special meaning behind it. He didn't mindlessly ink himself.

And he'd put me there. *Me*.

I'd have to decide where to get mine. I hadn't been kidding about that. I wanted one just like his. Maybe on my wrist? Oh, God. Dad would flip. I might be braver and a little bit more rebellious now, but not so much so that I'd go that far. It would have to be in a hidden spot. One Dad wouldn't have to look at. Maybe my hip?

I didn't know. All I knew was I needed one.

Just like I needed Finn to come back home to me, as soon as possible. I closed my eyes and for the first time in years…I prayed.

CHAPTER FOURTEEN

Finn

I shifted in the fake leather chair, tapping my foot in a rhythm that even I didn't recognize. All I knew was the longer I sat here, staring at the receptionist as she typed on her computer, the more impatient I got. If the receptionist sighed and clicked her mouse one more time, I might throw the damn thing out the window.

I'd gotten here at oh-eight-hundred sharp, but when I arrived on base, no one had known what the hell I was doing there. It wasn't a drill weekend—which I already knew—and no one else had been called in for duty. After a few phone calls, they'd sent me to this office, and I'd been counting fucking sheep in my head ever since.

Oh, and it wasn't *my* commanding officer who wanted to see me. It was Captain Richards who wanted me, aka *the* commanding officer of the whole fucking company. For the life of me, I couldn't figure out what he might want. I checked my watch, frowning when I saw it was already noon. How long were they going to leave me here doing shit?

The receptionist sighed and clicked again, and I narrowed my eyes at her. She wore pearls and a gray dress, and those glasses that women seemed to wear when they wanted to look smart. Her red lips were pursed, and she tapped her manicured nails on the mahogany desk.

The inactivity was getting to me. I didn't do sitting well, and I'd been sitting all damn morning. I was *this close* to lying on the floor to do a round of push-ups when the office door opened.

Captain Richards stepped out, and I stood at attention, saluting him and waiting for him to speak to me first, staring straight ahead at nothing.

"Sergeant, thank you for coming on your off weekend," he said.

I didn't move a muscle. "Good afternoon, sir."

Captain Richards studied my posture before stepping to the side. "At ease, sergeant. You may come in."

"Thank you, sir." I relaxed fractionally and nodded to him as I headed his way. "And I'm more than happy to be at your service."

Even if I had no clue what that *service* was.

He followed me in and shut the door behind us, making his way to his desk. "Well, you're probably wondering what you're here for." Captain Richards sat down behind his desk, motioning for me to sit in the wood chair in front of it. "And why I wanted to see you."

I perched on the edge of the chair, keeping my back straight. "I will admit to a certain level of curiosity, sir."

"Tell me, sergeant." Captain Richards rested his elbows on his desk and steepled his fingers. "Do you like being a Marine?"

"Of course, sir."

"Excellent." He tapped his fingers together, really slowly. "Where do you see yourself in ten years?"

Well, if that wasn't a loaded question I'd never heard one.

A few months ago, before Carrie, I would have had an easy answer. I'd be a Marine, and I'd still be guarding Senator Wallington. But now? It wasn't so clear-cut. In ten years, I'd hopefully still be with Carrie. Maybe we'd be married? Shit, I didn't know.

And more importantly? Why the hell did he care?

I cleared my throat. "I would imagine I'll be working in security, sir. Maybe something to do with computers. I've been thinking about getting my degree."

"What is your MOS now?"

"I'm a mortar man, sir."

"A grunt." He arched a brow. "So you want to go from infantry to a commissioned officer? Is that correct?"

"It's quite possibly my goal, yes, sir." I shifted in my chair, clutching my knees. "I've recently re-evaluated my life, sir, and am in the midst of trying to figure it out."

"Ah." His jaw squared off. "What caused this re-evaluation, if I might ask?"

My heartbeat thumped in my ears, louder than drums. "Sir? Why do you ask, if you don't mind my asking?"

His eyes narrowed on me. He was pulling rank on me. I knew it before he even opened his mouth. "Answer my questions, and maybe I'll answer yours."

"Sir, yes, sir." I cleared my throat, hating the fact that I had to sit here like a puppet while this man interrogated me, but it came with the dog tags. Obedience. Discipline. Respect. "I met a girl, sir."

"Might I ask this girl's name?" The captain reclined in his seat and crossed his ankle over his knee. "I do believe I'm acquainted with her father."

I must've blacked out for a second. God knows I felt as if he punched me in the fucking chest. He *knew* Senator Wallington? Well, there you go. Now I knew why I was here. Her father knew and sent me into a situation where I couldn't possibly lie.

God damn it.

I tried to remain calm on the outside, even if I was flipping the fuck out on the inside. "You know the Wallingtons, sir?"

"I do. Carrie is a sweet girl." He looked out the window for a second, then turned those piercing brown eyes back on me. "I've known her since she was in diapers."

I nodded, but didn't say anything.

"You're probably curious how I know."

I shifted on the seat. "Yes, sir."

"Her father asked me to track you. To make sure you were doing your job." Captain Richards eyed me. "Do you feel you're doing a good job, sergeant?"

"I feel she wouldn't be safer with anyone else watching her, sir." I met his eyes, refusing to flinch or back down. "I would guard her with my life."

"Would you do that even if you didn't love her?"

"Yes, sir." I tapped my fingers on my knees, but made myself stop. "It's my job. I take that responsibility very seriously."

"So if you were to guard another young woman, one whom you didn't love, you would still guard her to the best of your abilities?"

I blinked at him. "Yes, sir. I would."

"I heard about what you did when Carrie was almost robbed. Those were some impressive moves."

My cheeks heated up. "I was simply doing my job, sir."

"My man came home right afterward to tell me how impressed he was." Captain Richards raised his brow. "Keep in mind, he's a black belt in karate, among other things."

I bit down on my tongue, trying to figure out where the hell he was going with this. "I'm flattered, sir."

"Does her father know you love her?"

I swallowed hard. "No, sir."

"Why not?"

"We're waiting, sir." I gripped my knees even tighter. "My father is about to retire, and Carrie and I decided to hold off until after the fact."

"Ah." He nodded, his lips pursed in thought. "You're afraid he will withhold funds from your father?"

"Yes, sir," I admitted, sweat dripping down the back of my neck and rolling under the collar of my cammies. I wanted to yank at the collar, but I sat perfectly still. "That was our fear."

"*Our* fear?" He eyed me. "Carrie is in on this?"

Should I deny it? I didn't want her to catch any flak for my lies. But this was a captain in the Marines. I couldn't fucking *lie*. It's not the way the military worked. "Sir, I'd rather not say."

He considered me. "You're protecting her?"

"Sir." I didn't say anything else, but I didn't need to. My point was clear. I wouldn't be saying another word against the woman I loved.

He chuckled under his breath. "You know, I think he would approve if he saw you protecting her from me of all people."

I inclined my head. "Is this why I'm here, sir? Are you going to tell him about us before my father retires?"

"What?" He shook his head. "No. He doesn't know about you. But *I* do."

I wanted to ask him how or why, but it wasn't my place. This wasn't the civilian life where I was entitled to answers. Here, I got them if and when I deserved to hear them. "You're a smart man, captain."

"Indeed. You know what else I know?"

I'd *love* to fucking know. "Sir?"

"I believe you love her, and would do anything to protect her." He leaned forward again. The man was more fidgety than a fucking teenager. "Somewhere along the way, you fell for her, and she fell for you. Am I right?"

I tensed. It was none of his business. "Sir."

"You don't have to treat me as an enemy, son." He stood up and walked over to the window. "I have a proposition for you."

"I'd love to hear it, sir."

I wanted to get up and pace as I waited, but I sat on the chair like a fucking invalid. And worse? I felt like one. This man knew all of my secrets, and he didn't hesitate to air them in front of me like dirty laundry.

"Did you know how hard it is to get out of the infantry? Lots try, but it takes a hell of a long time and a lot of letters of recommendation."

"I did know it wouldn't be an easy move, yes."

I bit down on my tongue to keep from asking what his point was. If I couldn't make the move, then I'd get out. Go civilian. I'd thought it through. I had a plan.

I wasn't an idiot.

"I can help you make the move you need. One signature from me, and you're moving up the ranks." He leaned against the wall and crossed his arms. "It would be a simple matter."

I stiffened. I think I had an idea where this was going. "Sir…"

"Your unit is up for deployment soon," he said, cocking his head. "You will go overseas, away from Carrie, if you don't accept my help."

"I'm flattered and honored for the offer, sir," I said through my teeth. "However, with all due respect, I'd like to hear the cost of this favor before I accept."

Because everything came with a price.

And if he said what I thought he was going to say, it would take all my self-control not to punch him in the mouth, fucking C.O. or not.

He nodded. "You're a smart boy. I like that about you."

"Thank you, sir," I said stiffly.

"The cost isn't much." He uncrossed his arms. "Stop seeing Carrie."

I stood up, rage making me see red. I'd known—*known*—this is what he would say, but it didn't stop me from wanting to punch him in the fucking face. "No, thank you, sir."

I only made it one step to the door before he spoke again. "Don't you dare leave my office without leave, sergeant. You will hear me out. Sit *down*, boy."

I clenched my fists and turned back, sitting even though I didn't want to. "With all due respect, sir, I will not accept those terms. I will stop seeing Carrie if she asks me to. Other than that, I am not open to discussion."

"Not even to advance your own life?"

I clenched my fists so tight if hurt. "Not even to *save* my own life, sir."

"Good." He sat back down, his lips pressed tight. "Now that that's out of the way, let's move on to the real proposition."

I blinked at him. "Sir?"

"I wanted to make sure you really love her before I offered you this opportunity." He picked up his coffee mug, which said World's Best Daddy on it, and took a sip. "You obviously do, so I feel comfortable in offering you the chance of a lifetime."

"You're saying you were *testing* me?"

"Indeed. And you passed." He set the mug down. "Now we can talk business."

I stood up again. "Sir, what do you want from me?"

"I want you to *sit down*."

For a second, I considered walking out. Not sitting. But the years of military discipline wouldn't fucking let me. So I sat. "*Sir.*"

"I'll tell you everything. It involves doing something similar to what you're doing now, but with a huge reward."

"And what would that be, sir?"

He pursed his lips. "You'll find out. But first?" He picked up a pen and shoved a piece of paper at me. "Sign on the dotted line."

I eyed the paper. "I don't sign anything without reading it first, sir."

"Then by all means, read it." He leaned back in his chair and crossed his fingers over his stomach. "I'll wait."

I picked up the paper, scanning it quickly. By the time I was finished, I looked up at him, my eyes wide. This was a mission. A huge mission I didn't think I should be reading about, hence the top-secret security clearance application I could see sitting on the desk. "Sir, is this what I think it is?"

"It is. And I can give you all the knowledge you need to pull it off if you sign."

I picked up the pen, hesitated, and signed on the line.

CHAPTER FIFTEEN

Carrie

Saturday evening I shoveled more food onto a man's plate. I usually came to the soup kitchen on Sundays, but I was trying to keep myself as busy as possible. This time I'd dragged Marie with me. Speaking of which…

I met her eyes from across the room. She made a face at me and I nodded discreetly. It was time to go. There were only a few people here and it was getting dark. It had been a heck of a day. I'd said goodbye to my parents and then studied English with Cory for a few hours.

I felt exhausted yet wide awake at the same time. It was time to get out of here, maybe grab a bite to eat, and try to get some sleep. I had no idea what to expect when Finn returned. Or what to hope for, besides him not leaving.

As Finn would say…*this fucking wait was fucking killing me.*

I took off the hairnet and smiled at the woman who ran the place, earning a wave in return, set down some McDonald's cards, and made my way to Marie. "You ready to go?"

She nodded and headed for the door. "I don't know how you do this all the time. It's depressing."

Deja vu. "It's not depressing. They're hungry and need food." I shrugged. "It's simple."

She rolled her eyes. "Well, now I'm hungry and need food, so feed me. Where are we going?"

I always went to Islands with Finn after the soup kitchen. It was weird not having him here with me. I missed him, and it had only been a few hours. What would it be like when he was gone? No, *if* he was gone?

"How about some Mexican?" I unlocked my car. "I could go for a quesadilla."

"Sure." She slid into the seat and pulled the mirror down, fluffing her hair. "If we go to that place on Pico, we could dance, too."

"Dance? Yeah. I don't think so."

Marie rolled her eyes and buckled up. "You need to lighten up, Carrie. There's nothing wrong with dancing."

"You haven't seen me dance," I pointed out. "You'd disagree if you saw me in action."

She laughed. "That bad?"

"*That* bad."

"Okay, no dancing then." She looked at me, her eyes shining with excitement. "Hey, we're going skateboarding next weekend. How about if instead of feeding homeless people, you come with us? It'll be fun."

"That does sound fun." I buckled up and pulled out of the parking lot. "Count me in."

After we ate, I was on the way home alone. Marie had run into some guy she'd been flirting with lately and had chosen to stay with him. It was a relief, almost. It felt good to stop acting normal when I didn't feel normal.

I felt stressed, exhausted, and way behind on life. And so freaking *tired*. Plus, I couldn't stop thinking about what Finn was going to find out this weekend.

The whole way home, I went over every possible scenario that could come up. He could be going to war. Or maybe he was getting a promotion. Then again, he could be in trouble. Or he could be getting re-stationed across the country. The possibilities were endless, and I was driving myself crazy trying to figure out which one was the most statistically realistic one while also trying to figure out what my reaction would be.

If he had to move, would I move? Could I even do that?

I parked my car at the curb, not even realizing until I got out that I had gone to Finn's apartment. I'd been on autopilot…but since I was here, I could use my key to get inside and take advantage of the shower. This morning I'd woken up too late, and the line for the showers had been horrendously long. I hadn't had a good, hot shower in days, and I couldn't wait to feel the hot water running down my body.

I slipped the key into the lock, turning it and pushing inside without lifting my head from my phone. I had two missed calls. One from Marie and the other from *Finn*. My heart picked up speed as I kicked the door shut behind me, swiping my finger over the screen so I could listen to the voicemail.

But the voicemail wasn't from Finn. It was from Marie. Mexican music played in the background. *"Hey, it's me. I just wanted to let you know I won't be home tonight. Enjoy the empty room."*

I dropped back against the door, the disappointment at missing Finn's call so heavy that I couldn't stand it. I hugged the phone to my chest, tears filling my eyes. Why hadn't he left me a message? Even a simple *I love you* would have been better than nothing. "Damn it."

"What's with the cursing?" Finn asked, his voice loud and clear.

For a second, I thought I'd called him and somehow put the phone on speaker, but he switched on the light, and he was standing there in his uniform.

"Finn?" I stepped closer but then froze, my heart racing and seeming to painfully climb up from my chest until it felt as if it rested in my throat instead of my chest. I knew that wasn't possible, of course, but I'd swear to it. "How are you home early?"

"They only needed me for a few hours," he said, his tone neutral. "So I came home and called you right away. I saw you pull up, so I hung up."

I knew his being home meant something to us. Something good or bad. But suddenly it didn't matter anymore, because he was *here*. And that's all that mattered, wasn't it?

I took a step toward him, then another. By the time my foot hit the floor a third time, I was running. I'm talking hair-flying-behind-you, full-on sprint. Finn took a few steps toward me and opened his arms. I flung myself at him full force, holding on to him as if he alone could keep me on the ground.

He hugged me close, his arms wrapping around me so securely I couldn't even move, and he kissed my temple. I pulled back, meeting his eyes, and forced a smile. "I'm so happy you're home early."

He smiled back at me. Even though he hadn't opened his mouth, I just *knew* he was going to say something I wouldn't like. I could feel his heart thumping, beating against my own almost in tandem. "Carrie, I—"

"*No.* Not yet."

And I kissed him with all the emotions I had bottled up inside me all this time. I didn't want to hear what he had to say. Didn't want my worst fears to become so utterly, horrifically, devastatingly *alive*. When I had been a little girl, I'd been terrified of monsters that hid under my bed. Now, as an adult, I knew the real terror lie in words and actions. In life or death. Not in scary, hairy, huge beasts.

I kissed him with a desperation I hadn't felt before, knowing if I stopped he'd tell me the words I didn't want to hear. All those silly fears I'd had over the years seemed so freaking pathetic in the face of what I was feeling in Finn's arms.

He moaned into my mouth and stumbled back, his hands supporting me. I knew I was attacking the poor man, but I couldn't stop. Not now. Not ever. When he broke off the kiss, his breathing heavy and his grip on me unbreakable, I dared a glance up at him.

"Ginger," he said. "We need to talk."

I forced a smile for him, my hands gripping his shoulders so hard it probably hurt him, but he didn't so much as flinch. "I know," I said, my voice breaking on the last word. When he shot me a concerned look and opened his mouth to talk, I pressed my fingers against his mouth. "No. Don't say it. Not yet. I need a drink first."

He kissed my fingers and nodded, his bright blue eyes latched on me. "Have I ever denied you something you wanted?"

I wanted to demand he not leave me. He'd promised to give me everything I wanted, hadn't he? But that wouldn't be fair. Even *I* knew he didn't have a say in whether he left or stayed. It was all up to men like my father. To the men in the government who sat behind their desks, moving men like Finn across the world like chess pieces.

I noticed the outline of his dog tags, so I gently grasped the chain and pulled them out from under his shirt. I scanned the words that denoted his name, social security number, blood type, and religion. I now knew he was O positive. What a weird way to find out. I didn't even know what the heck type of blood I had, but I knew his.

Oh, and he was Catholic. He'd never mentioned this before. But we hadn't talked about God much, besides when he'd told me surfing was his version of church. We hadn't gotten to that part of our lives yet, I guess.

Knowing that this was how they kept track of who was who felt so cold and impersonal. But then again, that's how life was, wasn't it?

"Carrie…"

"I *know*. I need a drink first."

He gave me a look, one that said he didn't like this not-talking thing I was doing any more than he liked giving me alcohol, but I stubbornly ignored it. I went into the kitchen, grabbing him a beer and me a wine cooler. After I opened them, I went back to his side and handed him his beer.

He took it and sat down on the couch, his eyes never leaving mine. Then he held it out to me. "To us?"

"To us," I echoed, tapping my bottle with his. I brought it to my lips and drank it, not even taking a breath between swallows. Finn threw me a concerned look and pried it out of my fingers before I could drain it. "Hey."

Finn cupped my chin and turned my head, forcing my face toward his. "Carrie. Look at me."

"I can't. I just…can't." I closed my eyes tight, scrunching them shut. "I don't want to do this."

"Ginger…" He pulled me into his lap. "I need you to *look* at me."

I rested in between his legs, but facing him, a leg on either side of his hips. I squeezed my eyes shut even tighter, like a kid terrified to open her eyes and see the monster looming over her bed late at night. I couldn't handle this. I wasn't strong enough.

Wait. Yes, I was. I had to be strong for him. He needed me to be strong.

I took a deep, shaky breath and opened my eyes, my chest moving far too rapidly and my heart echoing in my head so loudly it freaking hurt. I knew that I wasn't going to like what he had to say, and I knew I was going to lose it. Completely lose it.

I rested a hand behind his neck, directly between his shoulder blades, and the other on his shoulder. I nodded, knowing he was waiting. Waiting for me to be ready.

It's not that I couldn't handle it. I could. I'd just needed some time. And I loved him even more for totally getting this about me.

I nodded once. "Go ahead. Tell me everything."

CHAPTER SIXTEEN

Finn

I looked at Carrie, her blue eyes on me and so breathtakingly beautiful, and I clammed up. I had so much I wanted to tell her, but I wasn't allowed to. I could only give her a fraction of the details, and then in a few days, I wouldn't be able to tell her anything. I knew she wouldn't like that any more than I did.

Our relationship had been built on secrets and lies, and now I had to go right back to not telling her stuff. To keeping secrets. I didn't like it, but my eye was on the end goal. And it would be worth it once we got there. *If* we got there.

I closed my hands around the back of her waist, holding on tight in case she tried to bolt. I needed to hold her. "I saw an old friend of yours today. Captain Richards. Does the name ring a bell?"

"Yeah, he went to the same college as my dad. They've been close ever since. I think he's coming for our Christmas dinner we always do." She shook her head, watching me closely. "What did he want with you?"

"He had an offer to make." I hesitated. "There's something I have to tell you first, and please try to understand this isn't up to me."

She stilled. "What?"

I rubbed her back in big, wide circles. "I can't tell you all the details of what I got asked to do. It's got a high-security clearance—one I just obtained today—and I am legally not allowed to tell you everything I know."

She blinked at me. "I won't tell anyone."

"It doesn't matter. I'm not allowed to tell."

She nibbled on her lower lip. "Do you not trust me to keep a secret? I mean, I know I'm not the best liar in the world, but I could do it."

I cupped her cheeks. "Ginger, it's not that. I fucking trust you with my life. But it's my job, and I *can't* tell you. It has nothing to do with trust, okay?"

"Fine. Yeah." She nodded jerkily. It wasn't fine with her. I could see it. "I get it, but what *can* you tell me?"

"Captain Richards asked me to take on a special case. It will involve me leaving in two days."

"What? Why? *No.*" She gasped. "Where are you going?"

"Away." I flinched. "Out of the country."

Her eyes flashed. "Where?"

"I can't say," I said, closing my eyes. "That's part of the deal, Ginger."

She pushed off my lap and paced. "Seriously? I can't even know where or why? That's ridiculous."

"I can kind of tell you why." I stood up and grabbed her, stopping her in her tracks. "I'll be doing something similar to what I'm doing here. Protecting someone."

She looked up at me, her red hair falling behind her shoulders. "A girl?"

"Yeah." I let go of her and tugged on my hair. "I can't say who."

"Shocker," she said dryly as she covered her face. "I'm sorry, that was bitchy. But I don't get why you can't tell me."

I pulled her hands down from her face, squeezing them slightly. "Wasn't there ever anything your father was working on that he couldn't tell you about? A bill or a law?"

"Well, yeah." She blinked at me. "Lots."

"Did he tell your mom?"

She shook her head. "No."

"See? It's like that."

She sat down on the couch, but she didn't make a sound. She just sat there, her eyes staring straight ahead. I sat beside her and held her hand, letting her process it all, and tried to keep quiet for her. I needed her to be okay with this.

After what felt like fucking hours, she looked at me again. She looked so resolute and strong. "Tell me everything you *can* tell me," she said, her voice surprisingly steady.

"He knows about us." I rubbed her lower back gently. "He confronted me, and tried to bribe me to walk away from you. When that—"

She held up a hand. "He did *what*?"

"He offered me a prestigious promotion. Everything I wanted, if only I walked away from you," I explained, keeping my voice level.

"What did you say?" she asked, her eyes narrow.

"No, of course." My hand tightened on hers. "What do you *think* I said?"

"I don't even know," she said, her voice soft. "How did he find out about us?"

"You know how you thought someone was following us?"

"Let me guess. It was his guy?"

"Yep." I smiled at her and tucked her hair behind her ear. "Your father asked him to send a guy to watch *me*. To make sure I was doing my job and not lounging about my apartment all day. He started watching when we were in our fight." I cleared my throat and looked away. I didn't like to think about that time of my life. "So at first, he didn't see anything but me following you. But then…"

"We made up."

I nodded. "And he saw a hell of a lot, and reported back to Captain Richards."

"Oh God." She paled. "Did he tell Dad?"

I shook my head and grabbed my beer. "Nope. Because he has a plan for me, and it involves me leaving on Tuesday morning."

"Which is the part you can't tell me."

I took a long sip. "Right. Maybe afterward, but not now."

"How long will you be gone? Will he tell Dad after? What does he want from you? When will—?"

I chuckled and pressed a finger to her mouth. "I don't know. And no, he's letting us handle the when and how of telling your dad, but after this it'll be easier."

"Why?" she asked through my fingers.

I got all excited thinking about what I was going to get for just a few weeks of work. "He's giving me the opportunity to change my MOS and become an officer, no military hoopla or shit to deal with. Just a quick transfer. I can go to college, fully paid for by Uncle Sam, and enter any field I want after this mission is complete. I can *do* anything. *Be* anything."

She bit down on her lip, her blue eyes examining my face. "Are you sure this isn't a way to split us up?"

"I'm sure." I leaned back against the couch. "After this, your father will have no reason to object because I'm going to be a commissioned officer."

She forced a smile. "That's great, and I'm happy for you. I really am, but what will this mean to us?"

"I can go to college, here even. We can be together, and even better? He promised to make sure my father gets his bonus, no matter what."

Her fingers tightened on mine. "So no more lying?"

"I still want you to wait until I'm back to tell your father." I drank another sip of my beer, and she picked up her wine cooler with a shaking hand. "I don't want you to do it alone. Once I'm home, we can come clean. Tell him we're in love. No more lies."

Her eyes lit up for the first time since I'd told her my news. She licked her lips, not dropping my gaze. "How long will you be gone?"

"It's looking like I'll be home after Christmas. It's in the early stages, but I think it'll be January at the latest."

"That's…" She swallowed hard. "More than a month away."

"Yeah, but it'll pass fast, I'm sure." I grabbed her hands, holding them to my lips and kissing them. "And when it's over, we'll be free. We can be together, no guilt or deception. Just us, going to college together like normal people."

She smiled at me, but the tears in her eyes kind of ruined it. "That's great, Finn."

"You don't look happy." I kissed her hand again. "This is good. I know it sucks I won't be home for Christmas, but it's worth it. I'm doing this for us, Ginger."

"I know." She pulled free and placed her hands on both my cheeks. "And I love you *so* freaking much for it. For making this happen. I'm just scared. I can't…I can't lose you, Finn. I just can't."

Her voice broke off, and she pressed her lips together, tears streaming down her cheeks. My heart clenched in my chest. I'd been expecting anger about having to keep my whereabouts a secret. Maybe a fight. I hadn't been expecting *tears*.

Logistically, this move made sense. It would solve all our issues, and give me a huge pay raise and life change. A fucking gigantic one. I'd only be gone for almost two months, and then I'd be back, and we'd be free. It was a simple decision.

This was a good move.

"I don't get why you're crying. I'll be fine, babe. It's not as dangerous as war, I promise you that," I said, kissing her tears away. They were salty and warm on my tongue, and I couldn't fucking keep up with them. "Please don't cry."

"I'm s-sorry." She took a shaky breath and closed her eyes. "I'll stop. I'm being stupid."

I hugged her close, breathing in her scent. Her hair was hard against my cheek, and it smelled a little funky, but I didn't care. I just wanted her to smile again. "Carrie, if you're not okay with this…"

"I'm fine. We're fine." She smiled at me, even through the tears, and rested her hand over my heart. "I love you, and you made a good move. I just needed a second."

I swallowed hard, the emotions inside of me warring with one another. I let go of her and lowered my head, not wanting her to see the emotions that were probably quite clear in my eyes. If I didn't do this, then I'd only be deploying next year, which was a hell of a lot worse than what I'd be doing overseas now.

But that didn't make it any easier on her.

Her fingers flexed on my shoulder. "You will *not* die. Tell me you won't. *Promise* me."

My heart wrenched. "I can't make a promise I can't keep, Ginger. I couldn't even make it if I stayed here and never left my apartment. Shit happens. You know that, but this is a hell of a lot safer than getting shot at in the desert. I can tell you that much."

"Then I guess I'll have to take it." She picked up her wine cooler and took a long sip. "I'd rather you stay with me, but I accept you can't."

I pulled her onto my lap and buried my face in her neck, hugging her against my chest as best I could. I swallowed hard, my chest and throat tight. "I promise to be diligent and to keep myself as safe as possible. I promise not to be an idiot. I promise not to be a martyr. But most importantly, I promise to fall asleep every night with you on my mind, and wake up smiling because I'm lucky enough to have you in my life."

She kissed me. She tasted like tears and watermelon wine cooler. "I'm the lucky one, not you."

Ha. Not true. I gripped her hips tight. "So we're okay?"

"Yep." She took a deep breath. "I'll be here when you get back, and then we can move on. Be happy and normal. Right?"

I chuckled. "As normal as I can possibly be, sure."

"Which is not at all," she said, smiling at me and nudging me with her elbow. "Will you be able to call me? Or text?"

I nodded. "Yeah. Email, if nothing else, but you'll be going home soon, so we'll have to be careful. I don't want you to have to tell your father without me. I want to be by your side, holding your hand when he finds out."

"I'll wait for you," she said, meeting my eyes. "Don't you worry about that."

I knew she meant more than the words sounded at face value, and I loved her even more for it. "And I'll be thinking of you the whole time."

She gave me a shaky smile. "You only have two days to get ready to leave?"

"Yeah." I flopped back against the couch, and she curled up against my side. "I guess I should call your dad."

"He's still on the plane. They'll land soon."

I nodded. "I'm going to be busy getting ready to leave, but I want to make sure we make time for us before I go. Monday night, it's just you and me. Got it?"

She patted my chest. I wished I could see her face, but she had it buried in my chest. "You tell me when, and I'll be here. You know that."

"Maybe," I said, grinning and kissing the top of her head.

I could feel her smile against my chest. "Your favorite word, if I remember correctly."

"Nope." I hugged her closer, so at peace with my decision and the future that I felt like I was floating on a cloud. "I have a new favorite word now."

"Oh?" She rested her hands on my chest and looked up at me, all wide-eyed and softness. "And what might that be?"

"*Ginger.*"

She smiled up at me and pressed her lips to mine. As I slanted my chin and took control, deepening the kiss, I knew it would all be okay. I'd get through this assignment in one piece, and then she would be happy because I'd be here with her.

Her father would accept me, since I was now going to be a commissioned officer, and I'd also have the backing of one of his oldest friends. I'd been promised that, too. This assignment wasn't without danger, but I'd told the truth when I said it wasn't as dangerous as war.

At least this was short term, and I more than likely wouldn't get shot at…

More than once or twice.

But it didn't matter, because we had each other. We had love. And we had commitment. On top of that, I had the belief in my heart that we could survive this. Actually come out of the other side still happily together, as strong and steady as we were now. And if I managed to avoid getting killed over there?

Then *maybe*—just maybe…

We'd even get our happily ever after.

CHAPTER SEVENTEEN

Carrie

Monday afternoon, I closed my eyes for a second and took a deep breath. Right now, Finn was packing the last of his belongings, and I was going a little bit crazy. I know he thought this was for the best, and it very well might be true. But until he was home safe, and in my arms, I was not going to be okay with this. In fact, I was a mess.

A hot freaking *mess*.

Marie kicked me under the table. "Dude, are you sleeping over there or what?"

"Huh? No." I straightened and cleared my throat, then smiled at her. "Sorry. It's been a long couple of days on top of the late night."

And it had. Dad was scampering to find someone to watch over me while Finn was gone, and Finn had been a whirlwind of activity since the night he told me he would be leaving. He'd had to get a whole bunch of shots, and then the packing and the phone calls…

He was doing this for us. Trying to make our life easier. But right now, all I knew was my boyfriend was leaving to go somewhere dangerous, and I wasn't even allowed to know *where*.

My phone buzzed and I picked it up eagerly. It wasn't Finn messaging me. It was Dad. *Where are you?*

I'm having coffee with my roommate.

A few seconds passed. *Call me when you're home.*

I didn't answer, and Marie sighed again. "You're ignoring me for your man, aren't you? And when will you tell me his name?"

"I wish. It's my dad." I showed her my screen. "And I can't tell you. It's too risky. The less you know, the better."

"Ah." Marie read the messages and rolled her eyes. "It's all so secret and *hush hush*. You'd think you were dating Channing Tatum or something."

I laughed. "Channing has nothing on him."

"I wouldn't know," Marie said, frowning at me. "But since you refuse to tell me more, I'll politely change the subject. Are you going home for the holidays?"

"I am." I looked out the window, my eyes on the people walking by. They all wore sweaters and hats, but it was only in the low sixties. I missed the snow. The cold, brisk air. Even with all this mess with Finn going on, I was excited to go back. "Are you?"

"Yep. I leave the Friday after this one."

"Saturday for me." I swallowed hard and turned back to Marie. "Where are you from again?"

"Three hours from here," she said, smiling. "So it's not that long of a trip. You're from back East, right?"

"Yeah." I swallowed a sip of coffee. "D.C., to be exact."

"Ah." She laughed. "So you probably laugh at me when I put on a sweater out here, huh?"

"Laugh? Not exactly." I smiled. "But it's not cold to me, no."

Marie looked out the window, a far-off look in her eyes. "I've never really been in snow. We drove to Bear Mountain a few times, but it doesn't feel like winter when it only takes ten minutes down a mountain to get back into the spring, you know?"

"Yeah, I totally get it. I miss the snow." I stared down at my coffee. I was supposed to be going home *with* Finn, not alone. "I miss home, too."

"Me too." Marie cleared her throat and reached out to grab my arm. "Speaking of missing things, whatever happened with your man, anyway? I didn't get a chance to ask how things turned out after your parents came to visit."

She flopped back in her chair, her Starbucks coffee in between her hands. She wore light gray fingerless mittens that were super cute, a matching sweater, and a pair of curve-hugging dark blue skinny jeans. Her blonde hair was soft and clean, and she wore her glasses again. She looked flawless.

I looked down at my own baggy T-shirt and jeans and tried not to compare us. She looked perfectly put together while I looked…well, like a hot mess.

If we weren't friends, I might hate her.

"Well…" I took a sip of my drink and swallowed. "Remember that job I told you about? The one that might take him away?"

"Yeah."

I set down my skinny white chocolate mocha. "He's leaving tomorrow."

"Ouch." Marie flinched. "How long will he be gone?"

"Until after Christmas." I licked my lips and looked out the window, half expecting to see Finn out there watching me. "I don't really know, because he can't tell me. His work is kind of…secret."

"Oh." Her eyes went wide. "*Oh.* Wow. Like, a secret agent or something?"

"Yeah." I forced a smile. "Kind of."

"Does he wear a black suit and look all hot in it?" Marie leaned in. "Oh, and does he drive a Ferrari and wear sunglasses at night like a movie star?"

I laughed. "No, not all that. He wears suits sometimes, but he has a Harley. Not a Ferrari."

"Oh, that's even hotter." She tapped her fingers on the table and bit down on her lip. "Does he surf and have tattoos, too?"

I blinked at her. "Yeah. But…how'd you know it was him?"

"I saw you two together at the beach the other day." She narrowed her eyes on me. "You told me he was gay."

"Yeah…about that?" I leaned in and motioned her closer, as if I was about to impart a big secret. "I'm really a dude. That's why I didn't want to shower in front of everyone."

Marie burst into laughter. "Yeah. Sure. And I'm Kim Kardashian."

"Hey, it's possible." I leaned back and smiled at her. This was fun. I was glad I stopped keeping her at arm's length. Turned out, Marie was a pretty great girl. "You never know what I have under these jeans."

"I saw you changing, and I've seen your tits." Marie snorted. "You're a girl, and he's straighter than an arrow."

"Guilty." I offered her an apologetic smile. "Sorry I lied. We were kind of sort of involved at that point, but in a fight."

She waved her hand dismissively. "It's fine. If I had that man in my hand, I'd lie to anyone who asked about him, too."

"Thanks for understanding." I reached out and squeezed her gloved hand. "I'm glad we did this. I needed the distraction, and it's been great."

"You need distractions because Double-oh-Seven is leaving?"

I laughed. "Double-oh-Seven?"

"Yeah." Marie shrugged, a small smile tipping one corner of her mouth up. "It seems fitting, since I don't know his name."

"I like it."

"Good. Now answer my question."

"Yes, I need distractions." I sighed. "I mean, it's tough to accept all this. I don't know where he's going, or how long he'll be gone. I don't even know how much danger he'll be in…" I broke off, not continuing on. What more was there to say? I think I pretty much covered it all with that sentence. "So, yeah. I'm a bit of a mess."

"It explains the dark bags you have going under your eyes." Marie pointed at my face and moved her finger in a circle. "And the pale face, too."

"Is it that bad?"

"That depends." She pursed her lips. "Will you be seeing him again before he leaves?"

"He's packing now, but we're meeting at his place tonight. I'm supposed to dress up and be ready to be wined and dined."

"In that case? Yeah, it's that bad." Marie stood up. "We need to get going. If I'm going to make you look human and fuck-able, I'll need all the time in the world."

A surprised laugh escaped me as she tugged me to my feet. "Geez, don't sugarcoat it or anything."

"Honey, we don't have time for that." She looked me up and down. "We've got to get to work if we're going to make you look drop-dead gorgeous for your last night together. Are you in, or are you out?"

I followed her, clutching my coffee to my chest. "I'm so in."

After all…I *did* want to look perfect for him.

Finn

I shoved my T-shirt into the suitcase on my bed, then headed into the kitchen. I had lasagna in the oven, and a bottle of champagne on ice waiting on the table. I didn't like supplying her with booze, but this was a special circumstance. It called for a romantic dinner by candlelight…

Oh, shit. I forgot to light the candles.

I grabbed the lighter out of the junk drawer and lit the wicks, making sure not to get too close since I wasn't wearing a shirt, then stood back to admire my handiwork. The table was set, the food was cooking, and the champagne was ready to go. I had an artificial tree set up in the corner, and a few boxes of ornaments and lights ready to go. We'd decorate it together later.

All I needed was the girl, and she should be here any minute now.

My phone rang, and I crossed the room to see who it was. Her father. Fucking fabulous. I swiped my finger across the screen. "Hello, sir."

"Coram," he said, his voice tight. "I spoke to Captain Richards, and he assures me he set a man on Carrie for while you're away. He says you know this man? This Hernandez?"

"I do, sir." I sat down on the couch. I still had to get dressed in the suit I'd planned to wear for Carrie, but obviously her father needed a bit of handholding right now. I played with the strings of my board shorts. "He's a great guy. Excellent at his job."

Papers shuffled. "And you know him how?"

"We're in the same unit," I said, dragging a hand down my face. "And he's in security, too. He's basically the California version of me, sir."

Only he won't fall in love with your daughter.

"And he'll take good care of her?"

"Yes, sir. I wouldn't trust him if he wouldn't." I yawned and tried to hide the sound behind my hand. I was fucking exhausted, but I could sleep on the plane tomorrow. I'd be spending half a day up in the air, without much else to do. "He's good."

"All right." He sighed. "I guess she'll be coming home in a little while, anyway, so it's not too long without you there. And you'll be back in January?"

"I believe so, sir."

"You know…" Senator Wallington paused and cleared his throat.

"Arnold told me a little about your mission. Stay safe, son."

I blinked. Was that actual concern for my welfare I heard? That couldn't be possible. Could it? I nodded. "Yes, sir. I will."

"Good. Happy Thanksgiving and Merry Christmas. Keep me posted on, well, you know, your status." Papers shuffled again. "Also, call your father soon. He misses you."

I'd talked to him this morning. He'd sounded much better. Even though I had wanted to, I hadn't told him about Carrie. I'd gotten close, but I decided to wait until we told her father. He didn't need to be burdened with my secrets.

"Yes, sir," I agreed. "I will."

The phone clicked off, and I sat there blinking at it. That had to be the strangest conversation I'd ever had with him. I stood up, fully intent to go get dressed, but my phone buzzed again.

Jesus, what was with the calls tonight? I picked up my iPhone and glared down at it. I sighed and answered. "What's up, Hernandez?"

"I won't keep you long, but I have a few questions," he said, his deep voice coming through the line with perfect clarity. "Can I run them by you real quick?"

"Sure." I walked to the closet. "But make it quick. Carrie will be here soon."

"Right. So she knows I'll be staying at your place while you're away, right?"

"I'll tell her tonight," I answered distractedly. I'd left one suit unpacked, and I couldn't find it. Ah, there it was, behind my jacket. I pulled it out. "What else?"

"She surfs, but she's not supposed to surf without you?"

"Correct." I flinched. "Though I didn't tell her that part yet."

"Okay. Please do. I don't want to do it."

"I will," I said, yanking the tie off the hanger. "What else do you need to know?"

We spent five minutes going over her schedule, then Hernandez sighed. "Okay. I think I got it."

"It's easy. She goes to school. She studies. She shops." I snorted. "It'll be the easiest job you've ever had."

Hernandez sighed. "Why does she need someone, anyway?"

"Got me." I sat down on the edge of my bed. "She got kidnapped as a kid, so I guess he's more paranoid than normal. Honestly? She's fine alone, but don't let that fool you into thinking you can relax. He will want constant updates—and if you let something happen to her? You'll answer to me."

Hernandez laughed. "Down, boy. I'm on it."

"Good." I paused. "Thanks, by the way. I appreciate it, man. I can't go over there without knowing she's okay, ya know?"

"I do." Hernandez sighed. "Or, I guess I do. I mean, I'm not in love and never have been, but I heard it can be rough on the mind."

I snorted again. "That's putting it lightly."

"I'll take good care of her, bro. I promise." I heard him shut a door or a cabinet. "You go focus on the job, and keep yourself safe."

I hesitated. "If I don't come back…"

"None of that," Hernandez said. "You'll come back."

"But *if* I don't," I said, my heart squeezing tight. "Tell her I love her, and take care of her until she moves on. Okay?"

Silence. "All right, man. I will."

I nodded, my throat aching in a weird way. "Thanks."

"Go woo your girl now. All's well here."

I nodded. "Later."

"Later."

I hung up and stared down at my phone. I hadn't really thought about the whole danger involved when I'd agreed to this plan, but hell, *life* was dangerous. Just because I was going into a hostile environment didn't mean I was going to die.

A bus could hit me tomorrow outside my apartment, for fuck's sake.

Why start worrying about what might happen over there when anything could happen here? It was pointless. Life was life.

You lived, and if you were lucky? You loved and got loved in return. And then, no matter how safe you lived your life, when it was all over, you died.

Staying in California wouldn't change that.

CHAPTER EIGHTEEN

Carrie

I smoothed my short red dress over my thighs and blotted my lips together. Marie had spent more than an hour on my hair, and even more time debating the best makeup, shoes, and dress to wear. I *knew* I looked good, even if I felt like a wreck. I wouldn't let my fear over the future ruin what tonight could be. What it *would* be.

It was our last night together, and I was going to make the most of it.

I slid the key into the lock, took a deep breath, and walked inside. The lights were dim, and candles were on the table. The whole apartment smelled like Christmas dinner, and soft carols played in the background. A bare tree stood in place at the window, and Finn was nowhere to be seen.

A suit was laid out across the bed, next to his phone. I smiled and walked up to it, running my hands over the soft fabric. I knew how much he hated dressing up, so knowing he was doing it showed me how special he was trying to make tonight. He didn't have to dress up to make me happy, but he didn't get that yet.

That's all right. I'd have all the time in the world to show him that… once he came back. And he *would* come back. There was no alternative in my mind.

The bathroom door opened, and he came out with nothing but a towel on. He saw me standing there and froze mid-step, his gaze sliding up and down my body. "Holy shit, babe. You look gorgeous."

"Thank you." I walked up to him and ran my hands over his damp chest. "So do you. Screw the suit, just lose the towel and we'll be good to go."

He grinned and leaned down, kissing me gently before he stepped out of my arms. "Not happening. We're having the date I should have given you the other night."

I pouted. "But—"

"No *buts*." He dropped the towel, and my jaw dropped as I watched the back view. Hot damn, the boy was fine. I mean, I already knew that, obviously. But still. The way his butt curved from his lower back to his hard upper thighs? *Wow.* "We're doing this my way. It's Christmas Eve."

I blinked at him. "No, it's not. It's not even Thanksgiving yet."

He stepped into his boxers and shot me a disappointed look. "Look at the calendar on the wall."

"Okay…" I walked over to the Santa calendar and looked. He'd left the month open to December, and he had crossed off all the days up until Christmas Eve. My heart twisted and tears filled my eyes, but I blinked them away before turning back to him with a smile. "You're right. Silly me."

He grinned and stepped in to his pants. "It's okay. I'll forgive you this one time. But as soon as I'm all dressed, the festivities begin. We have a tree to decorate, presents to open…" He walked over to me and wrapped me in his arms, smiling down at me the whole time. "And, of course, some good old-fashioned holiday sex to partake in, too."

I rested my hands over his heart, which sped up as soon as I touched him. "Of course. I wouldn't miss that for the world."

"Let me get dressed." He leaned down and kissed me. "Then we'll check on dinner." He kissed my nose this time. "And after that we'll get started."

"Okay," I said, my voice cracking. This was all so sweet and perfect and so *Finn*. And I was going to miss him so freaking much. I swallowed hard as he turned away, sinking down onto the couch. He'd put out a bunch of tiny Santa figurines on the coffee table, and cinnamon potpourri, too. "You even got Christmas potpourri."

He looked over his shoulder at me. "Huh?"

"This stuff," I said, pointing at the bowl.

"Oh, is that what it's called?" He shrugged into his shirt. "It reminded me of what my home used to smell like when my mom was alive." He looked off toward the tree, his brow furrowed. "At Christmastime, she used to put out Santa figures, angels, and bowls of that smelly stuff all over the house. Even in my bedroom."

"She sounds like she was wonderful," I said, standing up and crossing the room to place my hand on his arm. "I bet I would have loved her very much."

"And, man, she would have loved you." He met my eyes, the far-off look he'd had earlier disappearing. But the sadness lingered, despite the smile he gave me. "When I was planning on how to make it feel like Christmas for you, the only thing I could think of was what she would have done. I copied it."

"I love it." I reached up on tiptoe. "It's perfect."

He curled his hands around my waist. "No, *you're* perfect."

He was wrong. He was the one who said and did all the right things. I was fumbling along, trying to act as if I wasn't a complete mess. I was probably failing miserably.

"What did she do for a living?"

"She was a teacher. Third grade." He buttoned his shirt, his hands steady. "She said that was the best age to teach because they were old enough to take care of themselves, but they hadn't reached the cocky, know-it-all stage yet."

I laughed. "That sounds about right."

"Do you want kids someday?" he asked, his voice deep as he buttoned his shirt. "Little Carries running around the house causing trouble?"

I snorted. "I think it's the little Finns that will be causing trouble. Not the Carries. And yeah, I'd like two or three kids in, like, ten years maybe. You?"

His fingers froze on the second to last button. It wasn't until he looked at me, all heated eyes and *kiss me now* lips, that I realized why. I'd mentioned having kids *with him* instead of the fictional kids with my fictional husband. But when I pictured that life, I saw him at my side. I knew it. He knew it. Why pussyfoot around?

"I want two or three, too," he said, his voice raw and his eyes on mine. "And ten years is perfect."

I let out the breath I'd been holding and smiled at him. "It's a plan."

133

"It's taking all my control not to pick you up right now, throw you onto that bed, and practice making babies with you without actually making any." He finished up the last button. "But I have a plan on how tonight is going to go, you see. And I'm trying my best to follow it. So if you could stop looking so damn irresistible and stop saying all these things that make me want to kiss you, I'd appreciate it."

He curled his hand behind my neck and hauled me against his chest, and the breath *whoosh*ed out of my lungs right before he melded his mouth to mine, stealing all conscious thought. I closed my fists over his white dress shirt, wrinkling the material, but I didn't think he'd mind. Right now all that mattered was this. *Us.*

His mouth worked over mine and he pressed his hands to my lower back, his tongue gliding over mine perfectly. I moaned into his mouth and pushed him back against the wall. He went without a fight, but when I tried to start unbuttoning his shirt, he broke off the kiss and grabbed my hands. "Uh-uh. That's not supposed to happen yet."

I let out a small protest. At least, I think that's what came out. Maybe I just cursed. I didn't know, all I knew was I needed to feel his skin against mine. "We can go out of order, can't we?"

"Nope."

"*Finn.*" I slid my hands under his shirt, skimming over his hard abs, following along the top of his trousers, then dipped lower, barely brushing against his erection. "Are you so sure about that?"

His head dropped back against the wall and he swallowed so hard I could see his Adam's apple give way. "Nope…"

I stuck my leg in between his, liking the extra height these heels gave me. It let me brush my knee against the undersides of his balls, and when I did that, he groaned and flexed his fingers on my hips. He curled them around my sides and cupped my butt, yanking me even closer.

Then he kissed me again, and I was lost.

He backed me toward the bed, his lips never breaking free of mine. As he kissed me, his mouth moving over mine with a hunger he seemed to have lost control of, his hands roamed under my dress, skimming the top of the thigh-highs Marie had insisted I wear tonight so "nothing would get in the way."

She'd been right. That was an excellent move.

We fell back on the bed and I closed my legs around his waist, whimpering when he pressed against my core, rolling his hips ever so slowly. I tried not to focus on the fact that this would be the last time I'd get to have him like this for more than a month, but it was hard to do that when it's all I could think about.

This whole scene was romantic and *perfect*.

But it was still a bittersweet goodbye, no matter how sweet it might be.

He slid his fingers in between my legs, tracing the line of the panties I wore before slipping underneath them. He ran his finger over me, breaking off the kiss. "That day you came over without wearing any of these? That was fucking hot. From now on, I'll spend half my life trying to figure out if you're wearing anything underneath your clothes, and the other half finding out."

I scraped my nails down his back. "I'll keep changing it up then, so you'll never know."

"Jesus, Ginger." He nibbled on the side of my neck, then swirled his tongue over my pulse. "Are you trying to kill me?"

I shook my head. "Never that."

First, I undid the top button of his shirt with trembling hands, then the next and the next. The whole time I undid his shirt, he kissed me. My neck. My shoulder. My jaw. Anywhere and everywhere that he could reach without moving, he did. I had my legs around his waist, holding him in place, so he only had so much to work with…but *man*, did he make it work.

"Ginger," he murmured in my ear, rolling his tongue over my earlobe. "This strapless dress you're wearing is perfect, and you look un-fucking-believably gorgeous in it, but it's gotta fucking go."

He tore free of my death grip and stood, urging me onto my stomach before I could so much as say *get back here*. He bit down on my shoulder and I groaned, gripping the comforter. His fingers found my zipper and he slid it down, slow and agonizing. He kept dropping kisses over my skin as he bared it, and it was driving me insane with want.

By the time he reached the bottom, I was quivering. He nipped the skin right over my butt, his teeth sinking in just enough to sting. "*Finn.*"

"Yeah, babe?" he asked, dropping to his knees behind me and shimmying the dress down to my feet. "You need something?"

"You." I pressed my thighs together. "I need you."

He skimmed his hands up the outside of my thighs, then kissed the same spot he'd bitten, only on the other side of my butt. He ran his fingers down the backs of my thighs...and back up again. "Soon, my love. But not yet."

I shivered and buried my face in the mattress. How dare he ask me if I was trying to kill him? *He* was the one who was going to freaking kill *me*. He glided his fingers down my legs again, but this time he came up the insides. And when he reached the top, oh God, he finally gave me what I wanted.

He slipped his fingers between my legs, rubbing his thumb against my clit in slow circles. I whimpered and pressed back against him, wanting more. He flicked his tongue over the back of my thigh, quickening his strokes. I was so freaking close to what I wanted, but he stopped and stood up, leaving me high and dry.

"*Finn.*"

He undid his pants, let them hit the floor, and yanked his shirt over his head. "Don't move a muscle. I'm not done with you yet. But first..." He opened the drawer by his bed and pulled out a condom. "We need one of these since we're just practicing."

I grinned and wiggled my butt. "Hurry up or I'll get started without you."

"Fuck yeah. Do it."

My cheeks heated up. That had so been an empty threat. I hadn't actually been planning on *doing* it. I couldn't take it back now.

I rolled over and shot him a look that I hoped was more *seductress* than *deer in headlights*, and scooted back on the bed. When I was reclined against the pillows with nothing but my undergarments and a pair of heels on, I trailed my hand down my shoulder.

I felt stupid and ridiculous until I looked up at him and saw the way he stood there, his fists clenched and his gaze locked on my hand as it moved. Then I felt powerful. So freaking *powerful*. I bit down on my lip and moved my hand lower, tracing the curve of my breasts while he watched.

He ripped the condom open and pulled it out, his gaze latched on my hand as he did so. "Take off everything but the heels and the..." he said, his voice gruff. He gestured to my thigh-highs, "...the tights or whatever the fuck they're called."

136

I sat up and undid my bra, letting it fall to the side. Then I reclined back and closed my hands over my breasts, letting out a small moan. He took a step toward me, his blue eyes dark and his lips parted. "Jesus."

"Nope. Stay there," I said, not taking my hands off myself. This new strength I'd found was exhilarating, and if I was going to do this for him? I was going to do it right, thank you very much. His tattoo-covered muscles flexed when he stopped in his tracks. "No touching yet."

He curled his empty hand into a fist at his side. "You're touching."

"Only me." I rolled my hands over my nipples, licking my lips at the thrill that shot right to my core. Seeing him watching me do this was so freaking hot. "You'll get your turn."

He stepped closer and gripped his erection. "If you get to touch, so do I."

I looked down at his hand moving over his shaft and my stomach hollowed out. His abs clenched as his hand worked over himself and I moaned, sliding my hand even lower over my stomach. When I closed my fingers over my mound, he jerked his cock harder. Funny how I still blushed when I thought about that word.

I bit down on my lip and moved my fingers over myself, feeling the pressure building up even more so as I watched him touch himself.

He took a step closer. "Take off the panties, or I'll take them off for you. But if you make yourself come, with me watching, I'll blow your fucking mind right after. So I suggest you lose them."

I took them off in record time and pressed my fingers against my clit. I was so freaking ready it wouldn't take much to send me over the edge. I knew it. So I rubbed them in a circle, increasing the pressure when a jolt of pleasure hit me hard. "Oh *God.*"

"Fuck," he muttered, climbing onto the bed. He grabbed my ankle and nibbled on it, then kissed higher on my calf. "Keep going, Ginger. Show me how good you feel."

I whimpered and moved my fingers faster. Harder. "Finn…"

"I'm here," he said, his voice raw.

He slid his hands up my body and under my butt. Having him so close to where I was touching myself must have sent me over the edge, because I tossed my head back and forth and my entire body clenched. I increased the pressure, the pleasure and painful need ravaging me until I exploded, squeezing my eyes shut tight at the sheer intensity of it all.

I didn't even have time to crash and burn before he was in between my legs, his mouth fastening to mine and his erection pressing against my throbbing clit. All it took was one bump from him, and I came again—miraculously and explosively.

He deepened the kiss, his teeth digging into my lower lip, and then thrust inside me with one quick stroke. I closed my legs around him, digging my high heels into his bare ass, and clung to him for dear life. He moved fast and hard and heavenly. I wrapped my arms around him and dug my nails in, lifting my hips to take more of him.

The pressure was building up again, driving me higher and higher until I wasn't sure I'd ever be able to come back down. But then he swirled his tongue over mine and changed his angle, brushing against my clit, and I did crash down.

But first, oh my God, I soared. I freaking flew.

He thrust into me one last time, deep, before he tensed over me, breaking off the kiss long enough to utter, "*Carrie.*"

He made my name sound like a miracle or some amazing thing only he could have, and I didn't know what to say in reply. So I wrapped my arms around him and clung tight, squeezing my eyes shut. "I love you."

"I love you, too," he whispered, his face buried against my neck. He kissed me gently, right under my ear. "I'm going to miss you so damn much."

I swallowed hard. "I'll miss you, too."

It was almost funny. I'd been so high moments ago, but now I was back on the ground, and I didn't want to let go of him.

I didn't want to let go because I knew once I did...

He would leave me.

CHAPTER NINETEEN

Finn

I finished my lasagna pretty quickly and studied her from across the candlelit table. She was still eating, so she wasn't watching me like I was watching her. As a matter of fact, she hadn't looked up in a while. I knew why. She was sad I was leaving, and I wished I could take it back, almost. Wished I hadn't agreed to leave. But if I hadn't, then next year it would have been war.

I'd only have been delaying the inevitable. At least this way it was on my terms.

And once it was over, well, then I'd have Carrie. And I'd never leave her side again, if I had any say. I picked up my champagne and finished it with one swallow. I had to be up bright and early at five a.m. tomorrow, but I could indulge a *little*. No matter how I looked at it, or how many ways I tried to spin it into some bright shiny angle that would make me feel better, I was leaving the woman I loved behind. And I didn't fucking like it.

"You're awfully quiet over there, Ginger."

Her head snapped up and she swallowed her last bite. Picking up the cloth napkin with the Christmas tree on the corner I'd bought just for this dinner, she swiped it over her mouth and picked up her glass of champagne. After taking a hearty sip, she cleared her throat and smiled at me.

It was a strained smile. She was trying to hide how upset she was that I was leaving. "I was busy enjoying the dinner you made. It was delicious."

"Thank you. It's all part of the plan." I stood up and grabbed the bottle. I stopped at her side and wiggled it in the air. "You ready for a refill yet, slowpoke?"

"Usually you yell at me for drinking too much." She downed the rest of her drink and extended her arm, so I filled her glass and then mine. "Now you want me to drink more? Make up your mind."

In the background, Perry Como crooned on about a white Christmas. The flickering candlelight played with the shadows across her face. I smiled down at her and held out my free hand. "Well, tonight it's Christmas Eve, so the rules don't apply."

She slipped her hand into mine and I helped her stand. Once she was on her feet, I led her over to the bare tree. "Look up."

She did, her long, graceful neck arching as she did so. "Ah." She chuckled and tightened her hand on mine. "Mistletoe. That means we have to—"

I kissed her, not giving her a chance to say another word. When I pulled back, I rested my forehead on hers and clenched my glass tighter. "Kiss."

This moment right now? Fucking perfect.

"Mmhm." She smiled up at me, finally looking not so sad. "Are we going to dress this naked tree or what?"

"Of course." I dropped her hand and cleared my throat. "Do you want colored lights or white? I bought both because I wasn't sure."

"Mom only let us use white. She said it was more elegant, and that the future President of the United States deserved elegant," she said, her eyes latched on the tree. I reached for the white lights, figuring she'd want to make it like home. "So colored, please."

I froze, the white lights in my hand. "You don't want it the same?"

"Nope." She set her glass down and spun on me, her eyes shining. "We're not them. Why should we have the same things? I want cheeseburgers and beer, not caviar and three-hundred-year-old scotch. I want lasagna and mistletoe kisses, not press photos and chaste handholding. I want this. Us. And nothing you do or try to transform will change that. You make me happy. This makes me happy, and I love you so much for being *you.*"

140

The breath slammed out of my chest and I swear I might have staggered back, her honesty hit me that hard. She really liked me just like I was, and that fucking amazed me. "Then you'll have this every year. Anything you want, it's yours."

"I want you and only you." She curled her hands around my neck. "So come back home safely, or I might shrivel up and die."

My gut twisted and curled until I thought I might hurl all over her pretty dress she'd worn for me. The words were lovely and sweet, and I knew she intended them as such, but the thought of me dying and her being ruined by it made me sick. Fucking *sick*.

I'd never had someone depend on me like this. Need me like this. Not even my father. He'd be upset, but he would move on. She needed me, and *damn it*, I needed her.

I rested my cheek on the top of her head, which was a hell of a lot closer with those *fuck me* shoes on, and closed my eyes. "Sweetheart, I promise you that I'm not planning on going anywhere."

"Good." She rubbed her nose against my chest. "That's all I need to know."

I tightened my arms around her again. "Now let's get this tree decorated so I can give you my present."

"I don't have one for you." She nibbled on her lower lip. "I didn't know we were doing Christmas early."

"You don't have to give me anything." I kissed the top of her head and reluctantly let go of her. "You're all the present I need."

"I could tell you the same thing," she said, cocking her brow in a perfect imitation of me. "But you got me something anyway, didn't you?"

"That's different."

"How so?"

I opened the box of colored lights. "Because I want to spoil you rotten."

"So do I." She bent over and pulled out a white angel. "This is cute."

"You can't do that yet. It's last."

She turned to me, the angel perched between her fingers. "Says who?"

"Me." I pulled out the lights. "And, like, every single Christmas movie *ever* made."

She waved the angel under my nose. "Remember? No movies as a kid?"

"Poor, depraved child," I said, grinning at her. "Don't worry. I have the best Christmas movie in store for tonight."

"What's that?"

"*National Lampoon's Christmas Vacation.*"

She laughed. "It sounds interesting."

"Ginger, you have no idea." I handed her the end to the string of lights. "Hold that."

"I've never done this before." She frowned at the green corded lights in her hand. "Be warned."

I shook my head and squatted at the bottom of the tree. She was close enough that I had an interesting view up her skirt. I'd feel like a pervert staring up at her, but hell, she was mine and I was hers. I was allowed to look. "Just wrap it around like this." I wrapped it around the base of the tree. "And make sure you don't wrap yourself in it."

She rolled her eyes. "I'm not that bad."

"If you say so." I stood and wrapped the light around her legs. "Oops. Would you look at that?"

She burst into laughter and stepped free, her heel getting tangled in the little spot between the cords. "You're such a dork."

"You mean I'm adorkable, right?"

"Oh yeah. So much so." She snorted. "Help me out some more, will ya?"

We spent the next few minutes joking around and putting the lights on the branches. As I reached high, using the last of the lights, she stood back and wrapped her arms around herself. She looked happy enough, but she looked pretty damned sad, too. I bent over and picked up the plug. "You ready to see our handiwork?"

"Yes," she said, nodding at me with a smile. "Do it."

I plugged them in and crawled out from underneath of the tree. I stood up, brushing my hands off, and cringed. There was a whole spot in the front of the middle that had no lights. *None.* "Holy shit, we suck."

She turned her head to the side, squinting. "If you look really, *really* closely, you can see the extra lights we put in the back shining though the tree."

"Hm." I squinted and turned my head. She was right. I snapped my fingers. "I've got it." I crossed the room and slowly turned the tree. "Tell me when it looks best."

She tapped her chin and watched with all the scrutiny she would if someone had told her there would be a quiz later. Must be that attention to detail that would help her become an occupational therapist.

She brightened. "Right there. That looks good."

I stopped turning it and went back to her side. She was right. It looked perfect now. "Well, the window will get a bad view, but it looks good to me."

"Totally." She nodded decisively and headed for the couch. "Do you want the red balls or the green ones?"

"Green. Duh."

She laughed. "Sor-*ry*."

I slapped her on the ass, playful and silly. "The red ones are for my Ginger."

"And green are because…?"

"I like green." I shrugged. "I didn't really care what I had, only you."

"Is green your favorite color?"

"It used to be. Now it's the color of your eyes." I should have kicked myself in the nuts for that sappy sentiment. It sounded corny, but it was true. "They don't have a lot of blue ones, though. Mostly gold, silver, red, and green."

She swallowed hard and smiled. "Right. Christmas colors."

I hung an ornament, and watched her out of the corner of my eye. "My buddy Hernandez will be watching you while I'm gone."

She stopped with a ball half on the tree. "I hadn't even thought of that option. My dad's okay with it?"

"Yeah, he is." I guided her hand to the tree, urging her to hang the ball. "He'll be staying here so he can watch you close enough. I gave him a copy of the key earlier today."

She nodded and pulled out another ornament. "So no more free showers here, huh?"

"Nope. You'll have to slum it with the rest of the freshmen."

"Hey, that'll be you soon, too." She peeked at me out of the corner of her eye. "You'll be a grade under me."

"Fuck, you're right." I moved to the other side of the tree so we didn't get another bare spot. "You'll be robbing the cradle."

She snorted. "Oh yeah. Let me tell you."

Talking about the future made me feel a little better about what was coming tomorrow. We'd get through this and everything would be fine. We just had to keep the faith. I couldn't wait to enter this new life with Carrie at my side.

And I couldn't wait to be the man I knew I could be with her by my side.

If Captain Richards asked me where I wanted to be in ten years, I'd have an answer for him. I'd want to be right here, decorating a sloppy tree with Carrie. Maybe with a baby in my arms. That's where I wanted to be.

And I would be, damn it.

When we were finished, I guided her to the couch. After I had her seated and refilled with champagne—though I left mine empty since it was after midnight—I pulled out the long, skinny red box from the coffee table. It was next to my Glock, which Carrie was looking at with pursed lips.

"Are you bringing that with you?" she asked, swiping her hands across her dress.

"I am." I pushed it aside. I'd been cleaning it earlier, and left it out to dry. "It's kinda necessary in my job."

"You don't wear it here."

"It's not a hostile envir—" I broke off, realizing I was about to blurt out shit I wasn't supposed to. And she, of course, knew what I'd been about to say. "I mean, it's different."

She paled and bit down on her lip. "Right."

"Carrie…" I leaned forward and smoothed her hair back from her forehead. "Enough sad talk. Let's focus on this, because it's after midnight. That means it's Christmas Day."

She curled her hands into fists. "Merry Christmas."

"Merry Christmas." I pressed my lips to hers, savoring the kiss. Soon enough, we'd be falling asleep, and I'd be leaving. "Santa brought you a present."

She took the box from me, her gaze locked with mine. "I still wish I had something for you."

"You can give it to me after I come back. Now open it."

She nodded and ripped open the present. She ran her hands over the velvet case, her head lowered so I couldn't make out the expression on her face. When she flipped open the lid, she gasped and touched the pendant of the necklace I'd picked out for her.

It was yellow gold, and it had a sun hanging off the delicate chain. I shifted my weight, wondering if she'd get the significance behind the gift.

She looked up at me, tears in her eyes. "The sun's finally shining," she said softly. The tears that had filled her eyes just seconds before spilled over, and she threw herself at me. "I l-love it. Thank you."

I hugged her close, blinking because my eyes were stinging for some strange reason. "The sun will continue to shine because I have you. And you have me. Nothing will change that, okay?"

She nodded against my shoulder, her shoulders trembling as she cried. I held her close, making shushing sounds and saying words I didn't even pay attention to. Hell, I'd have promised her the moon and the stars if it would make her smile again.

Anything for her.

By the time she pulled back, her mascara was all over her cheeks and she was a wreck, but she'd never looked more perfect to me. I swiped my thumbs across her face, but I only smeared her makeup even worse.

"Want me to help you put it on?" I asked, my voice coming out strained.

She nodded and handed me the box. After I took out the necklace, she lifted her hair so I could clasp it on. After it was securely fastened, I kissed the back of her neck and she shivered. "Thank you," she said.

I nodded. "You ready for bed, or do you want to watch the movie?"

"Bed. I want to hold you until I have to let go."

My heart twisted. "Deal."

I led her to the bed and pulled back the covers, once we were naked, we made love. I held her in my arms until she fell asleep. The last thought on my mind, before I gave in to the overwhelming exhaustion that had been hitting me ever since I found out I was leaving, was that something that was this good couldn't possibly end badly.

We deserved our happily ever after, damn it.

Carrie

I didn't want to fall asleep. Didn't want to close my eyes. I lay there for a long time, my eyes on the cheery Christmas tree and my ears tuned in to Finn's even breathing. His arms were around me, and I had my ankle looped over his. It was heaven. How could I fall asleep when I didn't know how long it would be until I felt this way again?

My eyes drifted shut, but I forced them open again. I didn't want to miss a single moment of tonight. Wanted to cherish it. Hold it close to my heart in the upcoming weeks. My lids drifted shut again. I tried to lift them, but it didn't work. Maybe I would spend one minute resting them. I wanted to stay awake so badly. Wanted to hold him. Love him. Hug him. I wanted…

Him.

CHAPTER TWENTY

Finn

I brushed her hair off her cheek, my chest so tight I couldn't even fucking breathe. I'd already gotten dressed in my cammies, finished packing my last-minute stuff, and cleaned up dinner from last night so Hernandez wouldn't come home to a pigsty later this afternoon. She hadn't stirred through all the noise I'd made, proving how heavy of a sleeper she really was, but now I had to wake her.

All that was left was saying goodbye.

The hardest fucking part.

It was four forty-five in the morning, which meant my ride would be here in less than fifteen. It also meant I had to walk away from the one thing in this world that made my world brighter. I'd known it wasn't going to be easy, but I hadn't realized exactly how hard it would be.

The sun necklace I'd given her rested directly on the pale skin over her pulse, and all I could think was this was it. This was the beginning of a time when she wouldn't be with me, and I'd be off doing God knows what, while she was here without me.

There were so many things wrong with those sentences.

I leaned down and rested my forehead on her temple, my mind flashing back to the first time she'd slept over my house. I'd been dying to touch her, but unable to, and she'd been feeling the same way. I'd felt so desolate that I'd never get to have her, and now I had her, but I was walking away.

I breathed in her scent and kissed her on the tiny freckle under her eye, high on her cheekbone. "Ginger, I have to go."

"Hmm," she mumbled, rolling her head toward me but not opening her eyes.

She wasn't awake.

Part of me wanted to leave her sleeping peacefully. She was going to cry when we said goodbye, and all I wanted was to make her happy. So why should I wake her up to let her cry? But leaving without that goodbye didn't feel right either.

"Carrie," I whispered, kissing her lips gently. "I have to go."

"Go?" Her eyes fluttered open and she smiled at me for a fraction of a second before it faded away. That must have been when she remembered where I was going. "Oh. Oh God. Okay."

Her arms snaked around my neck and she held on so tightly what I could barely talk, let alone breathe, but I didn't protest. Why would I?

I needed her love more than I needed to breathe.

I hugged her close, burying my face in her neck. Walking away might be one of the hardest things I've ever done, but it would be worth it in the end. And if I kept telling myself that, then it would be true...ish.

I kissed the side of her neck, wanting to apologize for leaving even though I was doing what I had to do, and it would be okay. We'd be okay. "It'll be all right."

She nodded frantically, but didn't release her death grip on me. "I know. I just need a second."

I kissed the side of her neck again, since that's all I could reach with her stranglehold on me. "This isn't a goodbye. It's a see you later."

She made a small sound. "That's true. It's only, like, a month."

Actually, it was two. But I didn't feel the need to point that out. "Right." I pulled back to look at her, and she let me. I smiled down at her, trying to show her how calm I was about this whole situation so she'd feel at ease. "It'll pass by fast with Thanksgiving and Christmas...then before you know it, I'll be back here bossing you around, annoying you, and making you roll your eyes."

She let out a small laugh and her dimple popped out. Fuck, I loved that dimple. "You don't annoy me...too much."

"There you go sugarcoating things for me."

She kissed my jaw. "I don't sugarcoat. I tell it like it is."

"Oh, do you really now?" I turned my head and kissed her, keeping it sweet and gentle since my ride would be calling any minute to let me know he was here.

She smiled up at me. "I know this is going to work out in the end, and so do you. We'll skip the rest of the tears. Deal?"

I nodded slowly, smiling even though it fucking hurt. "Deal."

My phone buzzed on the nightstand, and I picked it up. "That's my ride. I've gotta leave now."

"Okay." She took a deep breath and kissed me. "I'll walk you out."

I pushed off the bed and slid my phone into my pocket. "If you want to."

"I do," she said, sitting up and sliding her legs over the side of the bed. She wore a pair of short shorts and one of my tank tops. She slid her feet into flip-flops, yawned, and reached out for my hand. She clung to me tightly, and I had a feeling I did the same thing to her. "Let's do this."

We walked to the door in silence, her hand entwined with mine. As I opened the door, I had to let go so I could wheel out my luggage. She picked up my laptop bag and slung it over her shoulder, and I let her because I could tell she wanted to help.

And if that's what it took to make her feel better, then so be it.

Carrie

I wanted to punch myself in the face right now. Anything to keep the tears at bay. I'd lectured myself so many times last night *not* to cry when he left, but it was getting harder and harder with each step we took toward him leaving. He didn't need to see me panicking and blubbering as he walked away.

He needed to see me standing there—strong and steady and *sure*. When he left, I could break down, but not a second before.

I straightened my shoulders and thought of anything I could think of besides the fact that my heart was being ripped out of my chest. My upcoming flight home. The lasagna last night. The way he'd held me all night long as if he didn't want to let go…

No. I shouldn't think of that.

Bad idea.

I followed him out the door, staring straight ahead and not meeting him in the eye. If I looked at him and he looked sad, I'd lose it. A black government-looking vehicle sat by the curb, right behind my car, its hazard lights flashing. That must be the car that would take him away to…wherever he was going.

I wasn't allowed to know. Stupid, stupid rules.

As we climbed down the stairs, each step felt heavier. Longer. Because each step we took would take us to that car that would spirit Finn away. I hated that freaking car with a passion. It represented everything I couldn't deal with right now.

We reached the bottom of the stairs and Finn set his suitcase on its wheels, then reached for my hand. I clung to it, knowing it was the last time I'd be able to do so until next year. He was my person. My rock.

What was I going to do without him here?

"You hanging in there, Ginger?" he asked, watching me with a furrowed brow. "If you want to go back up, it might be easier. Saying goodbye is never easy."

"It's not goodbye," I reminded him, smiling through the pain. "It's see ya later."

"Right," he said, his voice coming out rough. Oh God, if he cracked, I'd freaking lose it. Like, the nuclear warfare level of losing it. "I knew that."

We stopped at the side of the car and the trunk popped open. Finn wheeled his suitcase to the back and put it inside, then held his hand out for his laptop bag. I handed it off to him, our fingers brushing. He set the bag inside and shut the trunk with a *clunk*.

The sun was just starting to lighten the sky with tiny little tendrils of grayish-pink, and the birds around us were silent—still sleeping in their nests. It was just us and the guy in the car. And we…

We were out of time.

I held my arms open, and he closed me in his embrace, hugging me so tight he might have cracked a rib. I didn't care. He could take the freaking thing with him as long as he came home safe and sound. I cupped his cheeks and kissed him hard, squeezing my eyes shut so I didn't cry.

Not yet. Not now…

He pulled back and looked down at me, his bright blue eyes grave. Gone was the dancing blue eyes I loved so much. He looked sad, scared, and alone.

"Hey, none of that," I said, using his own words back on him. "I'll be here waiting for you when you get back, and it'll be over before we know it." I looked down at my hands on him, willing them to let go. To let him go. But my fists tightened on his shirt even as I told myself I had to do it. "Stay safe and write to me as much as possible, okay? And Skype if you can."

"I promise," he whispered, kissing me one last time. "See ya later, Ginger."

I forced a smile and let go. As he walked away, I wrapped my arms around myself and smiled at him so big that my cheeks were about to fall off. When he got to the car and opened the door, he looked back at me one more time.

I widened my smile even more and called out, "Hey, look. The sun's about to shine."

"Yeah." He looked up at the sky and let out a small laugh. "Yeah, it is."

With one last look at me, he got in the car and shut the door. The guy driving waited all of two-point-two seconds before he pulled away from the curb. A few seconds later, the car turned around the corner…and my Finn was gone.

As if in a trance, I turned around and walked back up the steps to his apartment. I'd go home later this morning, but right now I needed to be here. With him. Even if he wasn't here, it still smelled like him and his stuff was here and I needed to be, too.

I walked inside, shut the door behind me, and walked to his bed, my eyes barely blinking. As I passed the closet, I bent over and picked up one of his dirty shirts from the floor. Finn never left dirty shirts laying around, so it was like a bonus find. I held it to my face, breathed in deeply, and fell back into the bed.

I rolled onto my side, but on his side of the bed because I swore I could feel him there, his shirt pressed to my face. He was gone. Actually, truly gone. What was I going to do without him here, teasing me and loving me?

And now that he was gone, I could finally break down and feel the things that had been trying to kill me since he told me he was leaving.

Fear. Anger. Resentment. Fear. Love. Sadness. Fear.

It all crashed down on me, hard and fast, and I burst into tears. The pain and numbness—yeah, I knew that didn't make any sense—spread from my heart on out, slowly taking over my legs and arms. Even my fingers and my toes. I couldn't feel *anything* except the absence of Finn, and the fear he wouldn't come home.

I clung to Finn's shirt as if it alone had the power to make me feel better. It didn't. The only thing that would make me feel better was Finn, and he was gone. Just…gone.

What was I supposed to do with that?

CHAPTER TWENTY-ONE

Carrie

A few days later, someone knocked on my dorm door, and I put my history book aside, climbed out of bed, and answered it. Marie wasn't here, and I was catching up on some studying I'd been severely behind on lately. I had been missing Finn and crying myself to sleep.

It was the weekend, and I'd been dragging myself around with less than an hour of sleep per night for almost a week. Tonight I might break down and take a Nyquil or something that would knock me flat on my back. This no-sleep stuff was for the birds.

But first, I had to open the door.

I yawned, covering my mouth, and swung the door open. As soon as I could see who stood in the hallway, I cringed inwardly. It was Cory. He smiled at me and smoothed his light blue polo. "Hey, Carrie."

"Oh." I forced a smile. "Hey."

"We haven't talked in a while, so I thought I'd stop by." He paused. "Can I come in?"

I hesitated. Cory was harmless and all, but it felt wrong to invite him in when Finn wasn't here. "I don't know. I'm kind of a mess right now."

"You look fine to me." He looked me up and down, taking in my gray sweatpants and pink T-shirt. "What's wrong? You look upset."

That's because I *was* upset. Finn was gone. "It's been a rough couple of days." I stepped out of the way and let him in. "You can stay if you want, but I'm just studying. Nothing too exciting."

153

"Want to study and eat?" He looked at my open book, then at my bed. "You look like you could use a good meal. Or we could go do something fun for a change."

I stood in front of my bed. Should I sit down on it, or would that be weird? "I already ate. And I told you, I have to study."

"When's the last time you did something besides hang out with your boyfriend or study?" Cory asked. "I never see you around anymore. You don't go to parties or mixers. Don't hang out with any of us. It's like you don't exist."

I smoothed my hair self-consciously. Marie had been telling me I needed to go out and socialize, too, but I hadn't been in the mood. Was that so bad? What if Finn called when I was out? Or if he emailed me and…

Oh my God. I'd become one of those girls without even realizing it. I'd turned into a shell of the person I'd been. "I've been busy," I said a bit defensively.

"I know. We all have been, but we're about to all go home for the holidays. Wouldn't you like to have some fun first?"

I pictured Finn's face. He wouldn't like me going out with Cory. But he was here, and he had a point. I'd been a bit of a hermit. "I have a boyfriend."

"I know." He rubbed his stomach in a distracted manner. "I remember him quite well, actually. I'm not going to hit on you or anything. We'll just go out and eat."

"I don't know…"

"We can do something fun, you know." He grabbed my hand and pulled me to my feet. "Marie is going skateboarding with some guy she met the other week, at a place down the road. Want to meet up with her? That way it's not just the two of us."

Crap. Skateboarding. I'd forgotten that's what she was doing tonight. No wonder she kept trying to get me to come. I'd already said I would. It would be safer, too, since Marie was there. Going out alone with Cory felt wrong. "You know what? Let's do it. Let me get changed."

He grinned and sat down on Marie's bed. "I'll wait here."

"Okay." I dug through my clothes and pulled out jeans and a green shirt. "How long of a walk is it? Or should we drive?"

"Driving would be quicker."

"Give me five."

I left the room and headed into the communal bathroom, shutting a stall door behind me. Pulling out my phone, I texted Marie and confirmed she was skateboarding. Next I texted Hernandez—even though his name was Joseph, I could never remember to call him that.

Finn called him Hernandez, so I did. *Going skateboarding.*

He wrote back right away. *What is this, high school? And with who?*

Marie and some other friends. Cory too.

Coram hates him.

I rolled my eyes. *Yeah. I know. But it's fine.*

All right. I'm outside.

I set down my phone, got dressed, and fixed my appearance a little. I was out in less than five minutes. As I breezed back into my room, I called out, "Ready?"

"Yeah." Cory stood up. "And Carrie?"

I picked up my keys. "Yeah?"

"I know who you really are." He shoved his hands in his pockets. "Just wanted to put that out there."

I blinked at him. "What are you saying?"

"Carrie Wallington. Daughter of Senator Wallington, who is pro—"

I held up a hand, my heart thumping in my ears so loudly I could barely think. This wasn't good at all. If he knew, he held the power in our relationship. He could do anything he wanted, and I wouldn't be able to stop him. I swallowed hard. "When did you figure it out?"

"When they came to visit. I saw you out at the sushi place with them. I realized who he was, and I put two and two together." He shrugged. "Plus, you had security following you while they were here."

I closed my eyes. Dad and his stupid insecurities ruining everything. Now I had a potential blackmail situation on my hands. "Did you tell anyone?"

"No, of course not," he said, looking at me as if I'd hurt his feelings. "I wouldn't do that. You didn't tell me, or anyone else that I know of, so why would I do it for you?"

I studied him. He looked as if he actually meant it…for now. Would that hold true over the next four years? Maybe even more, if we went to the same grad school. I'd have to tread carefully from now on.

I gave him a small smile, trying to hide my suspicion behind a calm façade. If he knew I was freaking out, he would know how much power he held over me. "Thank you. I don't want people knowing about it."

155

"I figured." He took his hands out of his pockets and opened the door for me. "Don't worry. Your secret is safe with me."

I looked over my shoulder at him, trying to look as if I believed him one hundred percent when I *so* didn't. "All right. Let's go skateboarding."

Finn

I leaned back against the cracked wall, my computer on my lap. It was the first night in a while we were actually in a hotel instead of a fucking tent or some other shithole. This building was hardly the Ritz or anything, but it had walls and a roof and minimal bugs. I'd take it.

Plus, it had Wi-Fi. Fuck, I'd missed Wi-Fi.

I logged into my email, immediately opening Carrie's latest one. It was from last night at about midnight her time. I waited for the words to load, tapping my finger on my knee the whole time.

> *Hey Susan,*
>
> *I hope you're doing well. Guess what? I went out last night, despite my melancholy mood. You would've been proud of me. I went skateboarding—yes, skateboarding—with Marie, Cory, and a bunch of friends. I didn't even fall off...a lot.*
>
> *Can you believe that?*
>
> *When you get home, we should go. You'd like it.*
>
> *Well, it's after midnight and I'm sore and tired. Wear sunglasses today. I hear the sun is shining really bright.*
>
> *Carrie*

I closed my eyes and grinned, picturing her skateboarding with a big smile on her face. Not even the fact that she'd gone with Golden Boy could ruin my happiness for her. She was out living, even without me, and that made me happy.

I didn't think anything would make me happy in this shithole I was stuck in.

I pulled her picture out from underneath my pillow. The one I'd taken outside of my apartment a few days before I'd left. I ran my finger over the smooth surface and swallowed hard. Sometimes I wished I hadn't taken this offer. I could have been the one skateboarding with her. I could be holding her in my arms right now.

Shaking my head, I set her picture down and typed a quick reply. I only had two hours of down time, and I needed to catch some fucking zzz's.

Carrie,

Skateboarding, huh? That sounds fun…for a thirteen-year-old. ;)

I'm doing well here. Sunning every day. You won't even recognize me when I get home. That's how dark I'm getting in all this bright sunshine.

Get some sleep.

Susan

The door opened and I looked up. It was my roommate for the night, my superior, Eric Dotter. He rubbed his eyes and flung himself on to the bed next to mine. "Jesus, I've never been so fucking tired in my life."

I hit send and looked down at the twenty other emails I had—some from Dad, some from Hernandez—and sighed. I couldn't leave it open and disturb Dotter. "I hear ya, sir." I closed the lid to my laptop and set it aside. "I could sleep three days straight and not even roll over."

"I could do five." Dotter yawned, long and drawn out. "Nope. Make it six."

I settled back against the pillows, my hand going out to the spot Carrie was supposed to be. The bed felt foreign and empty. This wasn't where I was supposed to be, damn it. "Yeah, me too."

"We're going even deeper into the desert tomorrow than we did yesterday." Dotter heaved a long sigh. "Can you believe her? She's got a death wish."

"Yeah, and she's going to drag us all down with her." I tucked Carrie's picture under my pillow. "We've got almost two hours left. I'll catch you on the flip side of our night."

Dotter chuckled. "Good night."

"Night," I replied.

I laid there, looking up at the dark ceiling for a few minutes, willing my brain to shut down. It finally did, as Dotter's soft snores filled the room. But that's not what I heard as I drifted off. No, I heard Carrie's soft laughter as she climbed the rock wall on that day that felt like a year ago.

And I fell asleep with a smile on my face, despite the hell I was in.

CHAPTER TWENTY-TWO

Carrie

I leaned back against the car seat, my eyes focused out the window. Hernandez was driving me to the airport so I wouldn't have to leave my car there, and all I could do was sit there listlessly.

It had been close to two weeks now. Two weeks with no Finn.

I was absolutely miserable.

I kept going out of my way to live my life like normal. To not be one of those girls who was miserable because her boyfriend was gone. But my boyfriend wasn't away on a vacation or visiting home. He was away getting shot at or attacked.

I had nightmares about it every night, and I barely slept.

I'd tried to fill my days with activities. I'd studied. I'd even rock climbed and dragged Marie there with me. We'd skateboarded again a few times for fun, drank more coffee than was healthy, and even gone out dancing a few times.

Yeah. Me. Dancing.

Finn would never believe it, even though I told him every day what I did.

He always wrote back with encouragement and enthusiasm about my activities, but I felt almost guilty telling him the things I was up to.

While he worked, I danced and drank coffee. How was that fair?

Hernandez cleared his throat. "I heard from Coram last night."

"Oh yeah?" I sat up straight. "What did he say?"

"He thanked me for watching you and threatened my life if I failed in my job of protecting you." He shot me a grin. "You know, the usual."

I rolled my eyes. "He wouldn't actually kill you. He likes you too much."

"Um, I think he likes you more." He chuckled. "I don't kiss him or fu—" He broke off, his cheeks going red. "Well, you know."

"You can say dirty words in front of me," I said, my tone dry. He reminded me of how Finn was before we connected—all cautious and reserved. Ah, who was I kidding? He had never been cautious around me. "I won't tell my dad."

"I'm more worried about you telling Coram. I don't want him getting the wrong idea. You know?"

Like what? That we were flirting?

I looked over at him, eyeing him critically. I hadn't really paid him much attention, to be honest. He'd just been the guy who followed me around. The guy who wasn't Finn. I mean, he was nice and all, but we hadn't talked much.

He was cute. Really, *really* cute.

He had the same lightly tanned skin and dark hair that most men of Spanish descent had and dark brown eyes. There were tons of muscles and a few tattoos, just like Finn. He was a stunner.

If Marie ever saw him, she'd be all over him like white on rice. She loved exotic men, and he definitely fit the bill. Which got me thinking… "Are you single?"

He shot me a narrow eyed look. "Yeah."

"I have a friend. Her name's Marie. Blonde. Pretty." I tapped my fingers on the door. "Maybe when Finn gets back we can double-date or something."

"Uh…" Hernandez ran a hand over his short hair. "Yeah, maybe. We'll see."

I pulled out my phone. The home screen was Finn and me on "Christmas" night. I'd have to fix that before I touched down in D.C. I pulled up the picture of Marie at Starbucks the other day and held it out. "Here she is."

He stopped at the stoplight and looked, disinterest on his face until he focused on the phone. He leaned closer and grinned. "Okay. We'll do it once Coram's back."

"Deal." I laughed and shoved the phone in my purse. "Tell me, how did you two meet?"

He pulled forward and merged into the left lane. "At drill. When he moved out here, he told me how he was babysitting some spoiled little brat for a year." He shot me an apologetic smile. "Oops. Sorry."

"I know what he thought of me at first," I said, shaking my head. "It's not exactly news to me."

"I know. But then I asked for the whole story and all he would tell me is you were a politician's daughter and you'd never known a day of freedom in your life. We got closer over the weekend, and made plans to hang out the next weekend."

I nodded. "And then?"

"We met up for drinks and he said, 'Dude. I was wrong. She's not spoiled and I like her a lot. I'm fucked.'" Hernandez laughed. "I remember the look of panic on his face. He looked like he was in hell and about to fall off a ledge into the fiery pits."

I pursed my lips. "How long after he met me was this?"

"I think a week?"

"So we'd already kissed." I smiled. "Yeah, he was 'fucked,' all right."

"He told me about it. Told me he'd never met anyone like you but he couldn't have you." Hernandez pulled into the airport. "He also told me about your dad blackmailing him, basically, about his dad's pension. Did you know they've been friends for years? His dad and your dad? He begged Coram's dad to come work for him in D.C."

I blinked at Hernandez. "I didn't know that, no. If he's friends with Larry, why would he threaten to take away his bonus?"

"I think it's just that. A threat."

"You don't think he'd do it?"

"I don't know much about your dad. Just what I've gotten from his texts. But it seems to me that if a man begs a buddy to come out and work with him…" Hernandez turned the car off and gripped the door handle. "Then the last thing he'll do is take his friend's money. Right?"

I nodded. "You'd think so."

"I think your dad struck where he thought it would hurt Coram most. To make sure he would keep his hands to himself." Hernandez opened the door. "So he got Coram to agree to those terms."

I opened my door and got out, meeting Hernandez at the back of the car. "Yeah. Maybe."

"He's been very nice to me. Checks in a lot, but I already knew what to expect." He pulled out my luggage and set it on the pavement. "You have everything? Passport, ID, tickets?"

I patted my purse. "A politician's daughter never travels without that stuff. I got that drummed in to my head at a young age. Oh, and hey?"

He looked at me. "Yeah?"

"Thanks for taking me to Finn's guy for my tattoo. I can't wait to show Finn when he gets home." I pressed a hand to my hip. "It's his present."

He smiled. "Anytime. It gave me some ideas for my next one." He motioned me forward, my luggage behind him. "You walk, I'll pull."

We passed a military vet with a sign asking for a ride to San Diego. I reached into my purse and handed him some money and a gift card to McDonald's. "Good luck, sir. I hope you get home."

"Thank you, miss," the man said, squeezing my hand and smiling up at me.

Hernandez stood behind me, hovering close enough to grab me and protect me if necessary. "If you don't mind, I can give him a ride there after I leave," he murmured in my ear. "But it's your car."

I nodded. "This man will give you a ride, if you'd like. He'll be out in a few minutes."

"Bless you." The man shook Hernandez's hand. "Bless you."

Hernandez inclined his head. "I'm always willing to help out a fellow member of the military, sir."

After the arrangements were made for the man to remain where he was and wait for Hernandez to come back, we went into the airport. He shook his head. "Coram wasn't kidding about you wanting to save the world and everyone in it, was he?"

I flushed. "I wouldn't say that. I just like to help."

"You're going to school to be a therapist, right?"

"Yeah." I smiled and swiped my card down the slot for the baggage claim and ticket printout. "It's a good fit for me."

"I believe that." He set the baggage on the scale and watched as I checked in and paid. Once I was finished, he held out his right hand. "Well, have a nice trip. I'll be here waiting for you, if Coram's not stateside yet."

"Thanks, Hernandez." I shook his hand and laughed at myself. "I have to stop calling you that. Your name is Joe, right?"

"Yeah. Well, Joseph." He dropped my hand. "But Coram calls me Hernandez, so it makes sense for you to do the same."

"Well, goodbye, *Joseph*." I waved. "See you later. Don't forget about our double date."

"I won't." He pointed at me and backed toward the door. "Now get through that gate so I can give that guy a ride home. He's been waiting long enough."

I laughed and left, a smile on my face. He turned and walked out the door, his steps sure and powerful. He looked pretty darn good leaving, too. Even *I* had to admit it.

Marie was going to *love* him.

The next morning, I rolled over slowly, knowing when I opened my eyes that I'd be alone. Utterly, horribly *alone* in my parents' house. I closed my eyes, trying to hold on to how wonderful that last night with Finn had felt. I wanted to remember the way I'd felt after we made love—close and naked. And so freaking *happy*.

I did it every morning.

Then every morning, reality came crashing back down on me. It sucked.

I reached up and fingered the sun pendant I hadn't taken off since "Christmas morning" when Finn had given it to me. I still had no idea when he'd be home. I missed him so much it actually *hurt*. It was like I had this big, gaping hole inside of me that oozed pus and blood until I felt I couldn't go on anymore. I just wanted to hurry up through Thanksgiving and Christmas and get to the part when Finn came home.

My parents knew something was up with me. They kept bugging me and asking me why I was so silent, and I kept blowing it off. I wanted to tell them it was because I was missing a piece of me, but I couldn't.

I'd promised Finn I would wait for him, so I was. It still stunk.

Last night, I'd hung out with Finn's dad for a little while. He didn't know about Finn and me, but we used to hang out when I was younger, so he didn't question why I wanted to play chess with him last night.

He was trying to hide it from me, but I could see he was sick. I had a horrible feeling it was his heart or something like that. His skin was a pasty gray that couldn't possibly be healthy. Most of his duties had been delegated to younger men in the squad. Dad kept talking to him in low voices, and on top of that? He looked worried.

My dad. *Worried.*

If that wasn't bad, I didn't know what was. It made me want to demand he tell Finn, but I didn't have that right. Not yet. He might be fighting as hard as he could, but Finn deserved to know. I'd almost emailed him about it last night, but then I deleted it.

It didn't seem like something I should tell him over an email. We'd promised no lies or secrets, but I didn't even know for sure if his dad was sick.

I sat up and shoved the blankets down to my feet. I'd get an answer out of him soon, one way or the other. Tomorrow was the Annual Wallington Holiday Dinner, which was like Thanksgiving and Christmas rolled in to one. All of the house staff and security guards ate with the family at this party.

Dad and Mom always bestowed bonuses and gifts upon everyone, and the booze flowed freely. It was my favorite dinner of the year. As soon as my feet hit the floor, I had my phone in my hand. My heart skipped a beat when I saw I had an email from Finn. I opened it with excitement, eager for my dose of Finn.

Hey, Ginger.

It's hot here, and it makes me think of the cold ocean water in Cali. It's been a long day, and all I want to do is sleep, but I have to pull an all-nighter.

Remind me to show you my latest cheerleading move when I'm home. Camp's been fun because the sun is always shining.

See you soon,

Susan

I closed my eyes and fell back against the bed, my phone clutched to my chest. Every time I heard from Finn I relaxed for a few hours, because I knew he was alive and well. Then, a few hours later, I'd start worrying again.

But right now, directly after contact, was the highlight of my day. He was okay and so was I.

I smiled and typed a quick reply to him telling him I was sleeping well—even though I wasn't—and I told him it was sunny here, too. After I hit send, I nibbled my lower lip and looked outside. It was cloudy and gray and the snow was coming down so heavily you couldn't even see the driveway.

Sunny, indeed.

Last night, I'd asked Dad about his relationship with Larry—poked and prodded a little. Turned out Joseph—as I was now calling him in my head—was right. He and Larry *were* close friends. This only confirmed my suspicions.

Dad wouldn't screw over his friend. He might be a politician and controlling in a creepy way, but he wasn't that kind of guy. Dad wouldn't take away his friend's bonus. As soon as Finn came home, I'd tell him. It would remove one more worry from over his head.

I'd also found out some more about the commanding officer that sent Finn overseas—who was actually coming to dinner tomorrow night. He always did.

But Dad had been talking about visiting Arnold when he'd come to see me, and then he'd told me that Arnold was in charge of getting high-detailed security for important politicians and politicians' families.

Is that what Finn was doing over there…wherever over *there* was? Guarding a politician? That didn't sound too dangerous. I mean, it's what he did for me.

I liked the idea of him following some rich snob around Europe. It was safer than the nightmares that plagued me every night. A knock sounded at the door and I lifted my head to call out, "Come in."

"It's me," Mom said, peeking her head inside before opening the door all the way. Her faded red hair was pulled back impeccably in a tight bun, and her light green eyes sought me out. "Are you dressed?"

Her reactions never failed to make me smile. Did she really think I'd tell her to come in if I was naked on the bed? "Yeah, Mom. I'm dressed."

She came in and closed the door behind her. Tinkerbell, Mom's little terrier, whined from the hallway. "Tomorrow night's the Wallington Annual Holiday Dinner."

I almost rolled my eyes at how she used the *official* name for it, but held back.

"I know." I slipped my phone under my pillow in case Finn wrote back. I mean, he used the name Susan—he'd even created a *SusanCheers@gmail.com* account to stay in character—but I still didn't like to risk it. I sat up and hugged my knees, resting my chin on them. "Dad reminded me last night."

"I got you a new dress for it." She reached out and smoothed her hand down my head in the way she always did when I was upset. I was trying to act all happy and cheery, but it was hard when a piece of me was gone. "We're going to have some extra guests, too."

"Okay…" I rolled my head her way. "Who?"

"Arnold and his family, the Christensons," Mom turned her head and stared out the window, "and the Stapletons."

Why did that name sound familiar?

"Sounds nice." I wiggled my toes and sighed. "Do you need help setting anything up?"

She laughed, seeming to be relieved about something. "No, we hired temporary help so the normal help could relax before the big event."

Ha. Only in *my* life would that sentence make total sense.

Finn would've laughed at that, too. My heart panged, and the happiness I'd found moments before simply faded. "Mom, can I ask you something?"

"Sure." She crossed her legs and perched on the edge of my bed. "What is on your mind? Are you finally ready to talk?"

She wore a flawless pair of black dress pants and a light pink satin top. She looked every inch the lady. As a kid, I'd always wondered if I would turn out like her. If I would end up being soft spoken yet strong. Kind yet stern. Always the lady.

I didn't think I would anymore. It wasn't *me*.

"If I loved someone who wasn't from our normal crowd, would you approve?" I met her eyes, curling my hands over my calves. "If he made me happy, would you accept him?"

She pressed her lips together. "I don't know, dear. It would depend on the boy, I guess." She turned to me, bending and sticking her foot underneath of her thigh. "Why? Are you seeing someone you don't think we'd approve of?"

"No, not exactly." I shook my head. "I like a guy who isn't from our world. He's not a Christenson or a Wallington."

Mom nodded slowly. "Would he make your father's campaign look bad?"

"I don't think so, no." Finn's words echoed in my head. He'd said he wouldn't fit in on the stage with us, with his tattoos and his motorcycle, but I didn't care about that. "He's not a criminal or anything."

Mom sighed and rested her hand on my back. "Life is hard, and sometimes the heart doesn't make much sense. Sometimes it knows best, and other times it's wrong. You have to pay attention and decide when it's right and when it's off. If you're questioning our acceptance of this boy, chances are this time it's off and you know it."

"*Mom.*" I stood up and spun on her. "That's not true. It's not wrong."

"Are you sure about that?" She stood as well, remaining perfectly poised. "If you weren't uncertain, you wouldn't even have to ask. You'd just introduce us to this boy, and you'd be certain we would like him. Let's count the ways this doesn't add up."

"It's not that. I—"

"Hm. Let's see." She counted off on her fingers as she said, "Instead of telling us you have a boyfriend, you hide him and pretend he's not real. Then you ask me if I'd like him even if he wasn't one of *us*, whatever that means. Then you tell me the heart is right, even though it's not."

She had a point, but I wasn't hiding him because of what she said. I was hiding him because of his job, and because he wasn't *here.*

But I couldn't tell her that, could I?

"It's right and you'll see it." I put my hands on my hips. "When I'm ready to tell you about it, that is."

"I'll look forward to that time." Her chin lifted. "Until then, I'll assume we won't like your boy, because you won't tell us who he is." Mom sighed and walked to my side, not even narrowing her eyes or acting the slightest bit angry. "If he makes you happy, we'll like him."

I nodded. "Then get ready to knit us matching sweaters for Christmas."

"Good." She inclined her head toward my closet. "The dress I bought you is in your closet. I had Frances put it in there this morning."

"Thanks," I said stiffly.

She started to walk away, but then stopped again. "You know, I'm not a snob. You seem to think I am. I've just been around a lot longer than you have. I've seen a lot more than you, and I know how the world works."

"Maybe I want to change the world," I said, lifting my chin.

"Maybe you will."

And with that, she opened the door and left with Tinkerbell trailing behind her, like always.

CHAPTER TWENTY- THREE

Finn

I hated this fucking place. All I'd done for the past three weeks was eat sand, get shot at, almost get blown up twice, and miss Carrie. I walked around like some lovesick fucker who didn't know how to live without a woman at his side.

And even worse? I was *absolutely* that fucking guy. And this assignment sucked donkey balls.

I'd been given three hours of down time, and I had every intention of using it to sleep and dream of her—even if it *was* seven o'clock at night. When you only got a handful of hours to sleep on any given day, you took them when you got them.

I closed my eyes and tried to pretend I was with her. We were laying side by side, our hands touching and her ankle thrown over my calf like she always did in her sleep. Or maybe we were about to get ready for the big Wallington Annual Holiday Dinner.

I think that was today or tomorrow…

I'd kind of lost track of time lately. All the days blended into one long, drawn out nightmare. It would have been the perfect night to tell everyone we loved each other. We would all be together, with the normal social hierarchy gone.

We could have stood up, entwined hands, and announced our love for each other. I would look her father in the eye and assure him that I would never hurt Carrie…

Knock, knock, knock.

"Come in," I called out, sitting up straight and rubbing my eyes. Had I dozed off for a second there? It felt like it. "I'm up."

Dotter popped his blond head in through the crack of the door. "We're getting word of a disturbance up north about a mile. We have to go check it out."

I was on my feet within seconds, shrugging into my bulletproof vest. "Yes, sir."

He closed the door and I stomped into my boots, then grabbed my helmet off my bare bunk. I was halfway to the door before I realized I didn't have the most important item with me. I crossed the room and snatched Carrie's photo from under my pillow, tucking it securely inside my vest—next to my dog tags and over my heart.

As I walked out the door and nodded at my superior, he came to my side. "I heard a rumor we might be going home soon."

I stopped walking. "She's done exploring the rough and tough Middle East already?"

He snorted and opened the door. "I guess so. When she heard there was another disturbance she said maybe she would return home for the holidays. We might be stateside for Christmas."

I grinned. "That's the best news I've gotten all month."

"I hear ya, Coram." He slid into the Humvee and started the engine. I climbed up beside him, cocking my rifle and looking out the window. "Do you have a girl waiting for you back home?"

"Yeah." I closed my eyes for only a fraction of a second, picturing Carrie's sweet smile. I opened them when we pulled forward and onto the makeshift road. "You?"

"A wife and two kids." He drummed his thumbs on the wheel. "If I could be home for Christmas for once, I'd be quite happy."

"I'm sure they would be, too, sir." I scanned the shadows for any movement, but all was quiet on the western front. Okay, maybe that was a bad analogy to make when I was in this fucking place. "God willing, she'll realize she did enough pilgrimage and we'll be all set to go home for the holidays."

"From your lips to God's ears," Dotter said.

"I'm not seeing anything." I looked over my shoulder. "What was supposedly seen here?"

"We had a report of a suspicious blue vehicle, lurking by the entrance of the compound. And someone heard some loud booms." He shrugged. "Out here, that's not exactly the weirdest thing in the world."

"Damn straight." I kept looking. Nothing. "I think we can head back, sir."

"I think you're right, but, first, let's go west a little more."

I nodded and turned back out the window, watching for any signs of life. But in my head, I offered up a silent prayer that God had been listening earlier. That we were going home early, and that this nightmare would be over.

But most of all? I prayed we walked away from this fucking mess alive.

Carrie

The night of the party, I stood in front of the mirror and smoothed the maroon satin over the tulle that made it poof out underneath. Mom had picked the dress, and it *so* wasn't my style, but I wore it anyway. She'd gone through the trouble of finding it, so the least I could do was wear it once before I donated it to charity.

I looked at the necklace she'd bought for me to wear with it, but I didn't pick it up. If I wore that, I'd have to take off Finn's necklace, and that wasn't something I was willing to do. Not even for Mom.

I picked up the necklace she bought and shoved it inside the drawer by my bed. Then I went back to the mirror and studied my reflection. I looked tired and miserable. There were humongous bags under my eyes, and my cheeks looked hollowed out a little, too, no matter how much blush I applied.

But besides that, I guess I looked okay.

The dress was pretty. My hair was swept into a pretty updo that Marie had coached me through, and I had soft pink lip gloss on my lips. I picked up my phone and snapped a picture, then sent it off in an email to Finn.

He would like this dress. It looked easy enough to remove.

I waited to see if I got a reply, but none came. That wasn't a huge surprise. Communication from him was sparse at best, but I ached to get something from him. Anything. It was the only way I had of keeping track of him.

Of knowing he wasn't lying dead somewhere. I shook my head, trying to ditch that train of thought before it ruined my halfway decent mood. My phone buzzed and I picked it up, my heart racing. It wasn't Finn. It was Marie. *How's it going?*

I sent the picture I'd sent to Finn to Marie. *Good. Do I look okay?*

A few seconds, then: *Geez, girl. Have you slept AT ALL?*

Yeah. I tapped the phone on my chin. *Okay, not much. I miss Double-oh-Seven.*

As soon as I sent the message, I deleted it. She wrote back. *Ah. Well, it's almost over. Then we can have some girl time. For now, go to that party (I'm assuming you're going to a party) and have some fun.*

I smiled. *I'll try. Thanks for the pep talk.*

And SLEEP.

I tossed my phone on my bed and headed for my door. The guests would be arriving soon, and I had to be there to greet them, or Mom would have a heart attack. I walked down the carpeted stairs, my hand gripping the white bannister at the end in case my heels decided to slip on the marble foyer.

Dad turned to me and smiled wide, his blue eyes lighting up. He smoothed his graying hair and held his hands out to me. "Ah, it's my princess. Don't you look beautiful?"

"Thanks, Dad." I walked over to him, and he grabbed my fingers, squeezing them tight. "You look wonderful, too, of course."

He hugged me and kissed my forehead. His familiar cologne washed over me, and I hugged him, closing my eyes as I rested against his chest. "Thanks, princess."

"*Hugh.*" I heard heels come up behind me, and Mom said, "Watch the dress, you'll wrinkle it."

I looked up at Dad, rolled my eyes—which made him laugh—and turned to Mom. She headed toward us, Tinkerbell at her heels. Even the dog had dressed up for the occasion. She wore a red satin bow around her neck. "Well, you both look pretty. Very festive."

Mom wore a deep crimson dress that flowed to the floor in elegant swirls, and diamonds in her ears that would probably make the Queen of England jealous. She did a little twirl, her heels clacking as she did so, and leaned forward to kiss my cheek.

"So do you, dear," Mom said, smoothing her dress, even though it was flawless. Tinkerbell shot between her legs, tongue hanging out in excitement. "The first guests should be arriving soon. The house staff and guards are already drinking champagne in the dining room."

"Should I go in there with them so they're not alone?"

Mom shook her head. "No. You should wait here and greet our guests."

"Did you tell her that the Stapleton boy is coming tonight, Margie?" Dad nudged me with his elbow. "That's an *excellent* family if I do say so myself. Their son, Riley, is going to school in San Francisco."

Now I knew why I recognized that freaking name. That's the guy mom had been trying to marry me off to. No wonder she'd been so nervous when she mentioned their name yesterday. This was a setup. A date of sorts.

I turned to Mom and smiled, even though it probably looked more feral than kind. Her cheeks were flushed. "Oh, how *lovely*. I can't wait."

Dad patted my arm. "You'll like him. He has the same beliefs as us."

Then I probably wouldn't get along with him. But I didn't say that. "I can't wait," I said, smiling so wide it hurt my cheeks.

Laughter came from the dining room, and more joined in. The house staff and guards sounded like they were having a blast. I wanted to go in there with them and sneak a drink, but I forced myself to stand still. To play the part of dutiful daughter.

Soon enough they would see it was all an act. I loved them, and I was their daughter, but I wouldn't be their pawn. Not anymore. I pasted a smile on when the doorbell rang. Time to play the part.

"They're here," Mom said, clapping her hands excitedly.

"I'll open it, you two stand there." Dad headed for the door, his steps wide and sure. "Ready, girls?"

"Ready," Mom said.

They were acting like this was some huge thing, but we were standing here in dresses and heels like idiots. Even Tinkerbell stood at attention, for the love of God. This is why I'd never be like my mother. I felt like an idiot—and rightly so. I mean, why were we so freaking special that we were lined up like royalty on an episode of *Downton Abbey*?

It was *stupid*.

"Happy holidays," Dad boomed, clapping some gray-haired man on the shoulder. "Arnold, how good to see you."

I stiffened at the familiar name. He was the man responsible for sending Finn away. Even if he was helping, right now I didn't like him. His eyes clashed with mine over Dad's head. "It's a lovely night out for a party."

Dad nodded and laughed. "Indeed it is. Though it's not as nice as that California weather, is it?"

Arnold shook his head, his eyes still on mine. "Not quite. Right, Carrie?"

"Uh, right." I lifted my chin, raising my voice to be heard over Tinkerbell's incessant barking. "Nice seeing you again, captain."

He came to my side and dropped a kiss on my head. "I trust you'll be wanting to speak with me tonight?" he asked quietly.

"You'd be right," I gritted out. "After dinner."

"I'll meet you in the drawing room," he agreed, squeezing my hand before moving on to my mother. "Darling, you look fabulous."

I smiled and greeted his wife and two young children, then took a steadying breath. I had a lot of questions for him, but they would have to wait for now.

The doorbell rang again, and Dad opened it. Tinkerbell barked even louder. "Ah, hello, hello. Happy holidays," Dad boomed. "Come in. It's great seeing you again, Chris."

Chris. That didn't tell me which one this was. But then I saw the guy with him—young, tall, blond, and *really* hot—and I knew right away. It was the Stapletons.

My intended family…if my family had their way.

Dad beamed at me. "Ah, Riley. Carrie is home, so you won't be drowning in old people talk tonight."

"Sir, I must be old myself, because I've never been bored." He placed a hand on Dad's arm and met my eyes, his smile widening. He had dimples. Freaking dimples. "But I must confess, I'm excited to get to know you better, Carrie. I've heard so much about you."

I pasted on my generic smile and extended my hand, shaking his. His hand was rough and huge on mine, and he seemed friendly enough. If I had met him on this level before I'd met Finn, maybe he would have stood a chance with me. Unfortunately for him, he wasn't Finn. "I hope it was all good."

He laughed, deep and rumbly. Tinkerbell hopped up on hind legs, whining at his feet. Riley squatted down and pet her, grinning. "Indeed."

"Good." I bent over and whispered. "Then they were lying."

His smile slipped for a second, but he laughed and straightened to his full height again. Tinkerbell slinked back to Mom's side. "I think we're going to get along nicely, you and I." He held out his arm. "Shall we go get a drink?"

I made a face. "I'm not old enough."

"I won't tell," he whispered. "Come on, cutie."

I raised a brow. "*Cutie?*"

"Too soon?" He sighed. "I thought since we were getting along so well, we were there. Nicknames and all that."

"Uh…" I eyed him, torn between genuinely liking him, and not wanting to lead him on. He might be handsome and he might be a catch, but he wasn't mine to catch. My hook was already taken…or whatever fishing metaphor fit in this situation. I wasn't exactly the fishing type. I leaned in and dropped my voice. "Look, I have a boyfriend. My parents don't know about it, so they didn't tell you, but I do. Have a boyfriend. Who I love."

He held a hand to his heart, his other arm still extended to me. "You wound me. What part of my drink invitation said 'I'm looking to get into your pants'? I must've missed it, because I'd swear I simply asked you to keep me company in a dining room—not my bedroom."

I laughed, then covered my mouth. Mom looked over and smiled, obviously thinking her plan was working. "So you're *not* trying to get into my pants?"

"No, of course not." He skimmed his gaze over me. "Not yet, anyway. I mean, I just met you. Give a guy a little credit, will ya?"

I rolled my eyes. "Yeah, because not knowing a girl has stopped guys before."

"I'm not just any guy. I'm one of a kind. A Stapleton through and through." He put a hand on his chest, and for a second I thought he was serious, but he broke out in a grin and dropped his hand. "Was I cocky and serious enough? Did I pull it off?"

"Yeah, you almost had me." I laughed. "You're something else."

"I get that a lot."

I blinked up at him, fluttering my lashes a little. "From girls you flirt with?"

"I'm not flirting. I'm chatting, darling," he said, drawing out the syllable to sound snobby. "And while I'm sure you're quite lovely under that dress, I have a secret, too." He offered his arm again. "If you want to hear it, you have to follow me."

This time, I curled my hand into his elbow and let him. "Spill it, Stapleton."

He looked at me out of the corner of his eye. "Oh, you're bossy. I like that in a woman."

I sighed, but inside I felt alive. It had been so long since I'd gotten to relax and be myself. It felt *good*. "It comes part and parcel with being a Wallington."

"Ah, yes. I think I saw that in the informational packet your dad gave me about your blood lineage." As we crossed the foyer, he added, "Did you know my parents want me to marry you and make little trust fund babies? They made it quite clear."

I stopped walking and looked at him, my jaw dropping. "Uh, okay. That was a sweet proposal and all, but no thank you."

"Sweetie, that wasn't a proposal." He shuddered. "I am not my parents, and I have a feeling you aren't yours either. I'm betting you don't like being told what to do. Am I right?"

I bit down on my lip and nodded. "They told me the same thing—that I should marry you for the greater good."

"I'm shocked." He snorted and opened the door to the dining room. "Or not. But at least they're open and honest with us, right? They seem to forget this isn't the Victorian times, and we're not—"

"And we're not children who will do as they're told," I finished for him, smiling. I liked this guy. There was something about him that made me relax. "You're right, I think we'll get along great."

He nodded and picked up a glass of pink stuff, handing one to me. "Drink it before they come in."

"On it." I tipped it back and took a big gulp. It was fizzy and slightly sweet. And delicious. After I swallowed, I lifted my glass and pointed it at him. "You don't act like them."

"Neither do you." He took a thoughtful sip. "I think it's why we like each other. I mean, really, why am I in a tux for dinner with friends? How pretentious can we be?"

I giggled and took another sip. This stuff was even better than the wine coolers Finn always got me. I'd have to figure out what it was so we could keep it stashed at his place. "We hired help to replace the help. For *one* day. Like, what?" I held out my arm. "The house will fall apart in twenty-four hours?"

He rolled his eyes. "My parents are the same. When I'm done with college, I'm going to get a normal-sized house, a normal job, and marry a normal girl."

"They'll just die," I said fluttering my lashes. "Can you imagine the reaction?"

His gaze dropped to my mouth and heated, but then he looked away. "They'd have a heart attack, I'm sure."

I tried to ignore the look he'd given me. So what if he'd stared at my mouth for a fraction of a second? It didn't have to mean anything. And honestly, I didn't want to stop being silly with him. Ever since I came home, I'd been pretending to be something I wasn't. I wasn't the girl who left here all those months ago. *I* was different.

Finn had changed me, and I had no desire to go back to being that girl.

He took another sip of his drink, then grabbed both of us another one, stepping even closer to me. "Let's go sit over there. They'll think we're off flirting and maybe getting a head start on those trust fund babies, and we can drink. Maybe spend some time getting to know one another since we'll be married soon…"

"You *are* flirting with me," I said, narrowing my eyes on him. "The question is: why bother?"

"Dude, I'm respectful of the fact you have a man back in Cali," he said, his eyes drifting down my body. "But I'm not dead. I see a pretty girl? I flirt. Don't look too much into it. Although…wait. Scratch that. I *did* ask you to marry me."

I laughed and led him into the sitting room. "You're horrible."

"If our parents knew we were wandering off together, they'd be cackling with glee. I can picture them now, standing on the sidelines and rooting us on." He lowered his voice. "No, son, you have to move slower. Make it last. It's not a rush to the finish line, boy. Conserve your energy for round two. Stapletons *always* have a round two."

I choked on my drink and gasped for air. "Oh my God."

"Too much?" he asked as he sighed and leaned against the wall.

"Nope. It's just enough," I said, grinning. "You remind me of…well, my boyfriend."

He narrowed his eyes. "If you're going to ask me to stand in for him in a dark bedroom, I'll have to say…*yes*. Absolutely yes."

I rolled my eyes. "Yeah. Totally something he would say."

"He sounds like a smart guy." He finished his drink and sat down on the couch. "Come. Sit. Tell me about this paragon of a man."

"Well…" I took a sip and sat down next to him, setting my full glass down on the table next to his empty one. "He's a Marine. And he surfs. And rides a bike. And he's the sweetest guy ever. He treats me so…so great."

I broke off and played with the sun necklace. There weren't enough words to encompass all that was Finn.

"Mm." He tapped his fingers on the side of the couch. "Sounds like Mommy and Daddy will *love* him."

I snorted. "You have no idea, but I don't care."

"The heart never does," he said softly.

His words reminded me of Mom's, and all that "the heart is right or wrong" crap. I considered him. He looked awfully melancholy. "What about you? You have a girl back in San Francisco?"

"I did." He lifted a shoulder and offered me a twisted smile. "But we broke up when I found her in bed with her professor."

"Ouch." I patted his back. "Sorry."

"Eh, it's okay." He leaned his elbows on his knees. "It's not like she was *the one* or anything."

I pursed my lips. "Do you believe in that?" I asked.

"I do." He turned to me. "Don't you?"

"I do. I mean, I found him." I picked up my drink. "So I know it's real."

"I'm kind of jealous." He nodded. "Enough about me. Drink that and we'll go back in. It's time to act the part of the spoiled rich kids."

I finished my half-empty one and picked up the full glass, resting my chin in my hand. "You're so different from them."

"You are, too." He watched me, his green eyes sparkling with life and kindness. "I wonder why?"

"I…" I paused and tapped my finger on my lips. "I don't have a freaking clue."

He laughed. "Me either. Maybe it's the generation we've been born into."

"Yeah, maybe." I thought of Cory, who was the epitome of what my parents had to have been at my age. "Then again, maybe we're just freaks."

"Maybe," he agreed, laughing. "But the best kind."

I chugged the rest of my drink and stood up, smoothing my dress over my thighs. "You ready to go into the ranks again?"

"Yep." He rose to his feet and offered his arms. "Shall we?"

Such an old-fashioned phrase. I dropped into a curtsy, grinning up at him before taking his arm. "We *shall*."

I locked arms with him and we headed for the double doors that would lead us into the room where everyone—waitstaff, cook, house staff, and bodyguards—would be mingling with senators and governors. All dressed alike, all eating and drinking the same stuff.

We pushed through the doors and walked into mayhem.

CHAPTER TWENTY-FOUR

Carrie

Everyone was mingling and chatting, and the noise was incessant. Mr. Richards's kids were running around pretending to shoot at each other, and the conversation was deafening. I cringed and tightened my grip on Riley's arm. Suddenly, the empty sitting room seemed a heck of a lot better place to be. At least I could hear myself think.

Riley scanned the room. "Holy crap, this is insane."

"Yeah." I sighed and patted his arm. "Welcome to the Wallington Holiday Dinner."

"It's…different," he said, grinning.

"Ah, there you are," Mom said, smiling at me and then smiling even wider at Riley. "We were wondering where you two got off to."

Riley nudged me and I bit down on my tongue to keep myself from laughing.

"Oh, you know, Mrs. Wallington." He bowed at the waist. "Just talking and getting to know one another. Your daughter is fascinating."

"Perfect." Mom clapped her hands. "Come, come. There are refreshments of the spirited kind for you, Riley, and some sparkling cider and soda for those of you who aren't twenty-one."

I rolled my eyes. "Otherwise known as *me*."

"Yes, dear," Mom said, patting my arm. "Well, I'll leave you two young ones to yourselves as I mingle. Ta-ta."

I cringed and waved. "Bye."

"She's too cute," Riley said, smiling after her. "My mom is nothing like her. She's a bear disguised as a sheep."

I looked at his small, blonde mom. She looked sweet and rich, like the rest of the women in the room. She talked to her tall, gray-haired husband, while a few feet away Larry and Christy talked between themselves.

"If you say so. She looks harmless enough." I smiled at him and untangled myself from his arm. "If you'll excuse me, I'm going to go talk to some of the staff."

He bowed. "Have fun."

I nodded and made my way over to Finn's dad. He saw me coming and turned to me with a smile so much like Finn's that it hurt to see. "Carrie, doll. You look gorgeous tonight."

I smiled and hugged him. "You do, too. Very dashing."

"Thank you." He patted his thinning belly, sweat covering his forehead in a thin sheen. He looked exhausted. "I love these dinners."

"So do I." I pointed to an empty row of chairs. "Come, sit with me."

He smiled and followed me. "You're worried about me."

"You look tired is all," I protested. "Are you feeling well?"

"As well as a man my age can feel, yes." He sat down and stretched his legs in front of him, then turned his shiny blue Finn eyes on me. "Getting old is no fun, doll."

"I'm sure," I said, sitting down beside him. "Besides that…are you well?"

He looked at me, his brow furrowed. "I'm fine. I'm just worried about my son."

"O-Oh." I reached out and grabbed his hand, squeezing tight. "He's fine, I'm sure. He knows how to take care of himself, and I'm sure he wouldn't want you to worry about him."

God knows I'm doing enough of the worrying myself.

He froze and raised a brow, his eyes locked on mine. "Do you know him?"

"What?" I froze up, realizing what I'd done. I might as well have admitted to his father that I knew Finn and that we were dating. "I…I… no. I just meant that—"

"Carrie, dear?" Mom came up behind me and rested her hand on my shoulder. "It's time to sit down, so you'll have to follow me."

I swallowed hard, gave Finn's father one last look, then stood. "Of course."

As she led me away, I looked at Finn's dad again. He was watching me, his brow furrowed, and I know my heated cheeks were a dead tell, so I turned forward again. Mom led me to a seat that was next to Riley—of course—and next to one of the downstairs maids.

"You're here." She motioned Riley over. "And Riley, you're here."

I sat down, my heart thudding in my ears the whole time, and watched Larry as he sat across the table from me, but down a few chairs. Next to him was Mr. Richards, and they spoke to each other in low tones. I wanted to go sit next to them and eavesdrop, but I'd probably make a bigger mess out of it than I already had.

I stared down at my empty plate instead. I had a sinking suspicion that something bad was about to happen. It didn't make any sense, but I did. Maybe it was just paranoia about what I'd said to Larry. Maybe it was the drinks I'd had.

But something felt off.

"Hello, again." Riley sat next to me and waved his hand in front of my face. "Hello? Earth to Carrie? Are you in there?"

"Huh?" I looked up at him, blinking. "Oh. Yeah, sorry."

"You okay?"

"Yes." I nodded and picked up my water. "Got distracted for a minute."

He leaned closer, his hot breath washing over my ear. "Well, I am starving. Do you know what we're having?"

"Um..." I took a deep breath and scooted away. The light flirtation we'd been sharing felt a little too close now. Especially with my parents watching and scheming, and Larry across the table. "I think it's turkey and ham."

He nodded. "Excellent. I love them both."

"I hate turkey." I lifted my chin and stared at the table. "I prefer lasagna."

"That's good, too," he agreed. "I love lasagna."

"Is there any food you don't love?" I asked drolly.

"Um, nope."

I laughed and shook my head. "You're something else."

"I've been told that once or twice. By you even."

"By other women, too?"

"Of course," he said, grinning. "They all love me as much as I love food."

Such a cocky statement, but coming from him…it wasn't cocky at all. I had no doubt it was true. He was kind, hot, and smart. What wasn't to like? "I love food more than you."

"That's because you haven't kissed me," he said, shrugging. "That tips the scales in my favor."

I snorted. "Yeah. Sure."

"Care to find out?" he asked, raising his brow.

"I'll pass." I frowned at him. "But thanks for the offer."

"Suit yourself," he said. "Why isn't your boyfriend here, anyway? If I were your man, I wouldn't be sending you home alone at Christmas."

I took a second to choose my words carefully. "He's not—"

A phone rang, and everyone looked up. Then another phone joined in. I zeroed in on both the owners. Larry and Mr. Richards. Larry stood and fished out his phone, smiling at the table. "Sorry, I kept my phone on me in case my son called." He looked down at the screen and frowned. "Excuse me for a second?"

"Yes, of course," Dad said, nodding once.

Mr. Richards also answered, walking in the opposite direction of Larry. The two of them getting a phone call at the same time? That couldn't be a coincidence, could it?

My gaze darted between Mr. Richards and Larry, my heart racing and my palms going sweaty while my mouth dried out. Larry lifted the phone to his ear as he walked toward the double doors. If that was Finn, I wanted to know. No, I *had* to know.

I started to stand up, but Riley put a hand on my thigh. "*Dude*," I snapped, shoving it off. "Keep your hands to yourself."

"Whatever you're thinking about doing right now? Don't. Your dad is watching you and he looks *pissed*." Riley leaned in and smiled, completely at odds with his warning. "Something tells me you'd like to know about that call."

I took a deep breath and forced myself to sit back down. "H-How do you know?"

"I could see the tension in you when those men answered their phones," Riley said, picking up his glass of water. "And then the answering anger in your father. Who are they to you?"

"One's a bodyguard and the other is a family friend," I answered dismissively, stealing a quick glance at Dad. He was totally watching me, so I forced myself to look at Riley instead of Larry. "That's all."

Riley shook his head slightly. "If you say so."

A masculine cry sounded, and a phone hit the marble floor, clattering once or twice before landing. It was like a slow-motion nightmare. You know, the ones where a murderer is chasing you and you're running as fast as you can, only you're moving in slow motion? Yeah, that. Only ten times worse.

Dad was the first one on his feet, followed by me. Larry leaned against the wall, a hand to his mouth and his face even paler than before. I shoved my chair back and took off running in my heels, knowing I needed to get to Larry's side. Knowing I needed to help him, but also knowing he'd gotten bad news.

Bad news about Finn.

I bolted around the edge of the table. Mr. Richards grabbed my elbow even though he was still on the phone. "Carrie, wait. He'll know what's going on if he sees your face."

"*I don't care.*" I shook free, stumbling backward when he let go. "I'm going."

I took off again. Vaguely, I heard people shouting, and talking loudly, and Mom shouting my name, but I didn't even register any of it. All that mattered was getting to Larry. My throat ached with tears that were already threatening because I knew, I just *knew*, this was bad.

Dad got there first, and I wanted to shove him out of the way. "What is it, Larry?" he asked, throwing an arm around his shoulders. "What's wrong?"

"It's Griffin. He's been…oh my, God." Larry fell to his knees and scrambled for his phone with shaking hands, crawling forward on all fours. "I have to go. I have to go now."

"I'll take you," Dad said, squatting beside him and handing him the phone. "Larry, come on. Where are we going?"

I finally reached their side, but I'd already heard all I needed to know. I pressed a hand to my speeding heart, wondering how it could be beating when it had been ripped out of my chest just seconds before.

"W-What happened to him?" I asked, my voice barely more than a whisper. "Larry?"

"Larry's fine," Dad said quietly, standing up and smiling calmly at the people gathering behind me. "It's his son who's not all right. Stay here and control the madness with your—"

"*No.*" I grabbed the lapels of Dad's tux and shook him, then shouted, "What happened to Finn?"

Dad paled and gripped my hands. "Carrie…how…why…?" He turned red in the face. "*I knew it.*"

Larry stood up and started walking for the door. I didn't have time to waste trying to get answers out of Dad. I shoved off his chest and raced after Larry, grabbing his arm. The panicked rush of adrenaline was taking over my body, numbing the pain I knew would hit me any second. Right now I needed to *know*.

"Larry, tell me." I gripped him tighter. "Is he…is he…?"

I gulped in a deep breath and a sob escaped, so I covered my mouth. I couldn't even say the word. Not in the same train of thought as Finn. It wasn't right.

Larry paled and gripped my hands with his own trembling hand. "I don't know how bad it is. I think they said something about him being in surgery, but I dr-dropped the ph-phone."

I didn't know whether to shake him for doing something so incredibly stupid or hug him because he was obviously breaking. "Okay. Okay… we'll go there right away and find out. Where is he? Who called you?"

"He's in Germany. I don't know anything else," he rasped. "That's all I know," he repeated, his eyes focused on a spot on the wall. He looked like he was in shock, so I rubbed his back. "My boy. I don't even know…"

I nodded, trying to remain calm for Larry's sake, but inside I was freaking the heck out. This couldn't be happening. Not to my Finn. It had to be a nightmare. That was the only explanation. But I didn't wake up, and the pain wracking through my chest was all too real. I was awake. "Let's go find out more. Just let me grab my passport."

"No way, missy." Dad grabbed my upper arm. "You're staying here with your mother. I can handle this."

"*No.*"

"She can come," Larry said, his voice cracking. "It's fine."

My father stiffened and rose to his full height. "Carrie Louise Wallington, you *will* listen to me and you'll—"

"No, *you* will listen to me." I yanked free and glowered at him and everyone else who had huddled around to watch the show. Riley looked at me with sad eyes, and Mom was wringing her hands. "I am going because his son is Finn, and I *love* him."

Mom gasped and covered her mouth, her cheeks fusing with color. "*Carrie*. You don't even know him."

"Don't I, Dad?" I put my hands on my hips and stared him down. "Tell her why I know Finn, won't you?"

"Hugh? What's the meaning of this?" Mom asked.

"Oh for the love of God…" Dad said, covering his eyes.

"Carrie, go get your things," Mr. Richards said, laying a hand on Dad's shoulder. "I got this."

Dad yanked on his tie and threw his arms up in the air. "We don't have time for this melodramatic scene. Larry and I have to go. *She* is staying."

"*I* am going," I shouted. Tears were streaming down my face, and I didn't even care I had a whole freaking audience in front of me. "Do you even *hear* me? I love him, and *I* am going."

Larry grabbed my hand. "She's coming, and you can too, if you want. But we're going *now*."

Dad sputtered, his fists clenching and unclenching, then headed for the door without a word. I didn't have time to worry about him. I needed *Finn*.

He was okay. He *had* to be okay. Because if he wasn't okay…

I'd never be okay again.

CHAPTER TWENTY-FIVE

The town car sped down I-95, leading us to the airport. Dad had secured a private jet for the flight, and apparently he was going to Germany with us. He was going, despite his stony silence and glowers. All I cared about was getting to Finn.

"H-Hello?" Larry said, his voice soft. "Yes, this is him." Silence, then he sagged against the back of the seat and ran a hand down his face. "Can you tell me anything at all?" Larry nodded. "But how?" A moment of silence. "I…I see. Yes. We'll be landing at six your time." More silence. "Okay. Thank you."

He hung up and I reached out, grabbing his knee. "Tell me everything."

"There was an ambush. IEDs and guns…" He drew in a deep breath and covered his face with his hands. "He's in surgery, but I already knew that. They won't tell me anything else. They claim not to know." He dropped his hands from his face. "I think he's alive. I'd know it if he wasn't, wouldn't I?"

I didn't answer. I couldn't. I was too busy trying not to break down. We clung to each other's hands, not speaking. The whole ride to the airport felt like a nightmare. And the long plane ride turned out to be even worse.

I spent the whole flight praying and praying that Finn would be all right. But even more so, I prayed that this was all a dream. I was so sure I'd wake up in Finn's arms. He would laugh at me for being such a paranoid wreck, and I would snuggle in. I looked out the window and saw the clouds beneath us, and the pain hit me all over again.

It wouldn't leave me alone.

Dad swiped his finger across his phone. What was he doing, anyway? He couldn't be messaging anyone or doing something important since we were flying. I swear to God, if he was playing Candy Crush when I was dying inside, I'd kill him. He hadn't said a word to me this whole flight, but I didn't care.

I didn't have time for my daddy issues. Not when Finn…

God, he couldn't be dead. It wasn't possible. I had to believe, like Larry, that I would *know* if he was gone. I covered my mouth with my free hand, fighting back another sob trying to escape me. Wouldn't I know it, deep inside?

I had to believe I would, because the alternative wasn't acceptable. He'd left the country for me, for us, and now he could…he might be… *dead*.

And this was all my fault. If he died, that was on me.

After all, if he hadn't met me, and wanted to change for my father, he wouldn't have been offered that assignment. And he wouldn't have taken it. This had all been for us, and now he'd paid the ultimate price. While I…while I what? Dined and chatted with Riley, pretending I was single in front of my parents?

And why? All because he didn't fit in my world?

I was done. So freaking *done*.

I turned on my father, who was still staring at his phone. "He did this for you, you know," I said, a sob breaking up the last word. "He said you wouldn't accept him as he was, so he was trying to *fix* himself. Trying to make himself *better*. Are you happy now, Dad?"

Dad sat up straighter, the color draining from his face, but he didn't answer me. I knew what I was doing. I knew I was transferring my anger at myself onto my father, but I didn't freaking care. "Carrie…"

Larry squeezed my hand. "This isn't your father's fault, doll."

"Yes, it is," I said, sinking back against the plane seat. "It's his fault, and it's *mine*, too. Finn didn't think he was good enough for us. Didn't think my world would accept him. Well, I don't want a part in a world that doesn't accept a man like Finn. Not anymore. I'm done with it all. *Done*."

Dad finally broke his silence. "Carrie, don't be unreasonable. It's not like I knew about this. Griffin couldn't have known my reaction. He did this to better himself, not to better himself for me."

I laughed hysterically, then covered my mouth. "Don't you get it? He can't *better* himself because he's already perfect. He's the nicest guy I've ever met, but when you look at him, you won't see that. You'll see the tattoos and the motorcycle. Let's not pretend otherwise, especially not in front of Larry."

We all fell silent, and I closed my eyes. Tears rolled down my cheeks, but I didn't bother to wipe them away. What was the point? Nothing mattered until the freaking plane landed in Germany and we got to Finn. Until I got to see him. Nothing mattered until I knew whether he was still here with me.

The rest of the flight passed by with agonizing slowness, but I didn't break my silence the whole time. None of us did. We just sat there. Waiting. Hoping. Praying.

When we landed and got in the waiting town car, my mind was numb. And when the car pulled up in front of the hospital, after a series of ID checks and verifications, I was the first one out of it. I offered Larry my hand. He took it as he came out, holding on to it for support as we made our way in through the revolving glass doors.

Dad walked beside us, his tie loose, and his security behind us. I glowered at him. "You brought them here?"

"Yes, Carrie, I brought them here," he said, his voice tired. "They go where I go. And, as you obviously know, where you go, too."

I turned my head, not wanting to do this right now. Not able to do it. "Do we know where to go, Larry?"

"They said the third floor." He pointed at the elevator. "So I'm guessing we start there."

We walked to it in silence, holding hands still. By the time the elevator arrived, and we rode it to the third floor, I wasn't sure my legs would work anymore. But somehow, when the doors opened, I walked out. And then I took the steps that led us to the receptionist, who wore a scrub top with cartoon turkeys on it.

"Can I help you?" she asked, pushing her glasses up her nose.

Larry stepped forward and rested his hand on the desk. It looked casual enough, but I knew he rested on it for support. "Y-Yes, we're here for Sergeant Griffin Coram. We don't know if he's…"

When he didn't finish, instead covering his mouth and closing his eyes, I stepped forward and I squeezed his hand tighter. "If he's still alive, he means."

God, even saying that hurt.

The nurse's brown eyes flashed with pity, and she looked at her computer. "Go have a seat, and someone will be with you."

"Can you tell us anything?" Larry asked, his face pale. "Anything at all?"

She hesitated. "It's not my place to do so, sir. There's protocol and rules…"

"P-Please?" I added, catching her gaze. "Even something tiny."

She sighed. "He's here. That's really all I know. I don't know where or how he's doing. I don't even know if he's…living. I just see his name in the system—and that's all I can tell you."

Tears fell down my cheeks and I nodded, biting down on my lower lip. "Th-Thank you," I managed to say before I led Larry to his seat.

Dad followed, his fists tight at his sides. "That's bull. They can't tell you anything?"

"It's the way the military works," Larry said, collapsing in the plastic chair. "It's always been this way."

"Someone ought to fix that," Dad grumbled.

Larry and I both gave Dad a pointed stare, and then we all fell silent again. We sat there for what had to have been two hours before we saw anyone. A nurse in pink scrubs came up to us—her eyes empty and her face carefully neutral. "Sir? I can take you to your son now. The rest of your party will have to wait out here."

I stood up, almost falling over in my haste. "Can't I come, too?" I asked, my voice cracking. "Please?"

"Family only, ma'am," the nurse said, her eyes showing me she didn't want to refuse me. "I'm sorry."

I bit back a sob and covered my mouth. I didn't want to stay out here. I wanted to be with him. With Finn. "Okay. I'll wait here."

"You'll let her go back," Dad said, his voice clear and strong. "I'm Senator Wallington from the United States Senate, and that boy back there is one of mine. I'll gladly follow your rules and wait, but you'll let *her* go back."

I looked at him in surprise, tears still blinding my vision. "D-Dad?"

"Sir…I can't."

Larry rested a hand on her arm. "He'd want her back there. Whether he's alive or not…he'd want her there." He paused. "Please."

She hesitated, still gazing at my father, who stared her down until she finally nodded. "All right. She can come, but not for too long."

Not for too long? Did that mean he was alive? I was trying to dissect everything she said and it was driving me insane. When would they tell us something?

I looked at Dad, but he didn't look at me. Instead, he headed for the elevator without a word. Larry tugged me into the back room, and then we were entering a room with beeping noises and a lot of bright lights and…*oh my God.*

He was there. *Finn* was there, but he didn't look like Finn at all.

His head had white gauze wrapped all around it, and he had scratches all over his face, a black eye, and a bloody lip. It looked as if they'd shaved all his hair off, too. All I saw was skin, scars and stitches. There were stitches over his forehead that ran long and deep, extending underneath the bandage around his head. And he looked so pale. Almost as if…

As if he wasn't *alive*.

But the machine was beeping steadily. He had a heartbeat. He was alive.

I kept echoing that in my head.

I took a step closer, my own heart squeezing so tight that it hurt to move, let alone breathe. His eyes were closed, but his lips moved restlessly, as if he was having a bad dream or talking in his sleep. They were all scabbed up and dried out, and he looked as if he hadn't had a drink in days. His left arm was in a cast from the elbow down, and then a sling, too, as if it needed all the support it could get. His legs were covered with a blanket, but I didn't think he had any casts on underneath.

"Oh my God," I said, taking another step closer. "*Finn.*"

Larry cried out and rushed to Finn's side, and I watched as if I was out of my body. Unable to move or talk or do anything besides stare. I wanted to feel relieved that he was alive, but how could I feel anything resembling relief when he was in a bed—bloody and bruised and *hurt*?

The arm that wasn't in a sling rested at his side, but he had his hand fisted tight. As I watched, he loosened the fist, then tightened it again. He was holding something. I leaned closer, squinting. It took me maybe three seconds to recognize it. It was tattered, but I'd know it anywhere. It was the picture he'd taken of me outside his apartment. I hadn't even known he printed it out.

My gaze flew to his face, but his eyes were still closed. "I'm here, love," I whispered, even though he probably couldn't hear me. I stood there, not sure where to touch him…if at all. It didn't look safe to touch him anywhere. "I'm with you."

"Is he going to be okay?" Larry asked, his eyes on Finn. "Will he recover?"

"He's been confused and in pain," the doctor said. He walked to Finn's side and checked his vitals. "We've been keeping him dosed with morphine, and he's been pretty out of it because of that, so it's hard to tell what kind of effects the explosion might have had on his brain. We did an MRI, but we're still waiting on the results from that. With crude IEDs, you never know."

Larry covered his mouth. "What got broken?"

"He was lucky," the doctor said. "It was just his arm. Lots of bruises and stitches all over his body. There will be scarring on his face and his arm. And he got a concussion, as I said. We won't know the long-term effects until he wakes up. When his arm broke, the ulna came through the skin, so it was touch and go for a while. He lost too much blood before they could get him here, so he's weak. But he really lucked out."

I walked toward Finn slowly, my eyes on his cast. *That was lucky? How could that be considered lucky?*

"The rest of his unit died," the doctor said, watching me closely. "That's how he's lucky."

I hadn't even realized I'd said that out loud. I reached Finn's side, the one without the broken arm, and I slowly closed my fingers over his hand. I made sure not to crumble the picture, even if it was almost unrecognizable already. Even though he didn't so much as blink or wiggle his fingers, I swear…

I swear he *knew* I was there, and that was enough for me.

CHAPTER TWENTY-SIX

Finn

I kept seeing it over and over and fucking over again. The bright flashes as the IED went off. The deafening boom where I heard nothing at all, followed by me wishing I *still* heard nothing at all. The screams. The blood. The dead men...

Then there was my superior's leg getting blown clear off his fucking body, and then blood spurting everywhere, even in my face and burning my eyes. I swear I could still smell it. Taste it. I'd never forget that hellish night.

I'd tried my best to slow down the bleeding, even as it stopped squirting and just started to trickle slowly, I didn't let go. Even as his face went lax and cold, losing all traces of life. Everyone around us went into panic mode, shooting at anything that moved. I didn't let go until they dragged me away kicking and screaming.

And the pain...

God, it wouldn't fucking leave me alone.

I'd been fully conscious when my arm snapped in half and I flew from the Humvee, and I'd been so sure this was it. That I was a fucking goner. And in a weird, twisted way, I kind of wished I *had* died. At least then, I wouldn't be living through an endless replay of the attack in my mind.

I was fairly certain they had me doped up on some strong pain meds, so I didn't feel the pain. But yet…I did. Maybe I was dying. Or maybe I was already dead.

All I knew was that I was in *hell*.

I felt someone poking at my head, and a masculine voice talking about brain damage and possible long-term repercussions. I wanted to shove him off me and tell him to leave me the fuck alone so I could die in peace. I wanted to shout at the world, demanding they shut the fuck up. But then…

Ah, then I heard *her*.

I felt her soft hand touch mine, immediately calming me, and I tried to open my eyes. Tried to see if I was really dead, or if I was alive with Carrie at my side. If Carrie was here, I was alive. It felt unfair, almost. I knew no one else had made it out alive. Only me. I should have died. I really *should* have fucking died.

"Finn? Can you hear me?" Carrie's voice asked, the hand on mine tightening. "I love you. I love you so much. You've got to wake up for me. Open those blue eyes."

Either I was alive, or I was right and I was burning in hell, because I swear that was actually Carrie. I tried to open my mouth to ask her if she was real, but only a squeak came out. A small, pathetic sound.

"Oh my God, he's waking up," Carrie called out, holding on to me with both hands. Her grip on me hurt. That's how fucked up I was, but I didn't care. "Doctor Sloane, he's waking up."

I felt a man's hands probing me, then heard, "Be prepared for the worst. He might not remember things. Might not remember you two at all."

The fuck I didn't remember her. She was my Carrie. I managed to make my fingers move, and she cried out. "Larry, he's moving."

My father was here? But where *was* here?

"Son, I'm here with you." What I assumed to be Dad's hand fell on my arm, gentle and yet rough at the same time. He sounded fucking exhausted, and he sniffed loudly. "We're both here."

I managed to crack my eyelids open, but the bright lights shining down on me hurt, sending shards of pain through my brain. I slammed them shut again, then opened them more slowly. I blinked against the bright light and managed to turn my head *just* enough to see who stood by me.

Jesus Christ, I hadn't died. Carrie was here with my father.

She wore a short purple-ish dress, a pair of ripped tights, and her hair was falling all around her face. Her makeup was smeared across her cheekbones, and she had the hugest bags under her eyes I'd ever seen … but she was my very own angel.

"C-Carrie?" I managed to croak.

She burst into tears and nodded, smiling at me. Fuck, she looked perfect. "Yes, it's me," she said. "I'm here."

Dad gripped my arm and kissed the left side of my forehead. "You scared us, son."

I'd scared them? How had they even known about it? I had so many questions to ask, but I didn't want to. Not now. All that mattered was they were here. And I was alive.

Fucking *alive*. I wasn't sure how I felt about that yet.

Carrie kissed my hand, her hot tears hitting my skin. She blinked at me, a soft smile still on her lips. I knew she was putting on a show for me, trying to be brave and all that shit. And I loved her so much for it.

"I know you feel horrible right now, but I've never been happier to see those blue eyes," she said, kissing my hand again.

"You…" I took a deep breath. It hurt to fucking talk, but I had to say something to let them know *I* was still here, under all the scrapes and bandages. "Look like hell."

She blinked at me, then a surprised laugh escaped her. Dad chuckled, too, and I eased my head back on the pillow, closing my eyes. That's what I'd needed. Right there. I needed them to take a break from crying or worrying about me.

And it's what they needed, too, even if they didn't know it.

"I'm sure we do," she said, her voice still light.

"It's been a rough night, son," Dad said. "Not anything like yours…"

"I'm feeling pretty good right now," I said, trying to make light of the fact that I felt like I was dying slowly. "I'm h-h…"

My voice broke and I swallowed hard. I kept picturing the life leaving Dotter's eyes as I clung to his bloody stump of a leg. Jesus Christ. I'd never forget it.

The doctor cleared his throat. "I think we should let him rest now. I'm going to get him another dose of morphine. You'll have to say your goodbyes till tomorrow."

I tightened my fingers on Carrie. I'd just found her again. I didn't want her to leave, but the nurse pushed a button on my IV station, and the world spun in front of me, taking away my vision and even my concentration. "C-Carrie?"

"I'm still here," she whispered.

"Tell me something before they dope me up again," I whispered, urging her closer. "Before I'm g-gone."

I felt her move closer to me. "Yeah?"

"Is the sun shining?"

Her tears hit my arm, rolling off onto my hospital bed. "It is. And it won't stop. I'm right here with you. I'm not going *any*where."

I nodded and drifted off, the nightmare starting all over again. I could still smell the flesh burning, and I could hear the cries of the dying men all around me, but I knew I wasn't there anymore. I was home. And Carrie was here, too.

I'd be all right.

What might have been minutes or hours later, I opened my eyes again, blinking into the empty hospital room. I heard someone move closer and slowly turned my head, hoping to see Carrie. Instead, I saw her father. Senator Wallington.

For a second I thought I was hallucinating, so I blinked again. He was still standing there, watching me with those intense blue eyes. I tried to speak, but nothing came out. I was too damn high to make a fucking sound.

When he saw my eyes on him, he took a step closer and rested his hand on my bedrail. "I know you probably won't remember this, but you're a hero, son."

I blinked. Yeah, I was totally fucking high right now.

He sighed. "I know you love my girl, Griffin. And I know she loves you, too." He looked down at me. "I get why you fell for her. Who wouldn't? It doesn't mean I'm *happy* about it, though. Or that I'll accept it."

I wanted to reply so fucking bad, but nothing came out.

I swallowed and tried to open my mouth to talk, but the drugs were still dragging me down. All that came out was a moan sounding like, "*Sir?*"

He flinched and reached out, pushing a button on my IV that

controlled my morphine drip. "Get well, son. For both of our sakes."

Within seconds, the screams of the dying men took over my head again…

And I fell back into my own version of hell.

ACKNOWLEDGEMENTS

I have to first and foremost thank my family. My husband, Greg, for being so supportive every time I have to hunker down and get to work. And for my kids: Kaitlyn, Hunter, Gabriel, and Ameline…you're the best things I ever did. Thanks for being you.

I also have to send my love to my parents, sisters, nephews and brother-in-law. Thanks for being my cheerleaders and also for pimping out my books occasionally. I know you always have my back, and that's an amazing feeling.

And my amazing agent, Louise Fury from The Bent Agency. You've been my nonstop supporter, backbone, guide, and are just all-around awesome to be with. I don't know what I'd do without you there, helping me make the right choice. You're a rock star! Much love to you and your hubby, too.

To Team Fury, and everyone at The Bent Agency, I have to say it: I love you all. You're a great team to be on, and I thank my lucky stars I get to be a part of the group every day!

And thanks are also due to my fabulous publicist at InkSlinger PR, Jessica Estep. You're the best, and I couldn't possibly handle all these blog tours and blitzes without you. And thank you so much for all your excitement and confidence in this book, and in me.

I couldn't leave out my best buddies: Trent, Jill, and Tessa. You three are my rock, and I love how close we've gotten lately. NYC crew forever, man!

To my wonderful, fabulous, amazing critique partner, Caisey Quinn. You never let me down, and you're always here for me, no matter what. I love you, girl!

Thanks to Casey, as well, for your expertise in all things Finn. You're the best.

To my editor, Kristin; my copy editor, Hollie Westring; my formatter, Emily Tippetts; and my cover artist, Sarah Hansen: thank you so much for giving me the best quality service out there! I love you all.

A huge, huge thanks goes out to all the Carrie and Finn fans out there. Thank you for joining me for the second part of their journey. I hope to see you for the final portion of the journey next year!

And to all my writer friends…you know who you are. There are *way* too many to name in this small section, and I don't want to leave you out. You know I love you. You know how much you mean to me. And thank you for being you!

THANK YOU!

ABOUT THE AUTHOR

Jen McLaughlin is a New York Times, USA Today, and Wall Street Journal bestselling author. She writes steamy new adult books for the young and young at heart. Her first release, *Out of Line*, came out September 2013. She also writes bestselling contemporary romance under the pen name Diane Alberts. Since receiving her first contract offer under the pen name Diane Alberts, she has yet to stop writing. She is represented by Louise Fury at The Bent Agency.

Though she lives in the mountains, she really wishes she was surrounded by a hot, sunny beach with crystal-clear water. She lives in Northeast Pennsylvania with her four kids, a husband, a schnauzer mutt, a cat, and a Senegal parrot. In the rare moments when she's not writing, she can usually be found hunched over one knitting project or another. Her goal is to write so many well-crafted romance books that even a non-romance reader will know her name.

Lightning Source UK Ltd.
Milton Keynes UK
UKHW040624160519
342784UK00001B/26/P

9 780989 668415